PRAISE FOR MA
THE ETERNAL

"This fantasy earns style points for being set in modern Las Vegas—in a hotel whose residents include polar bears, giant Siberian tigers, and Princess Anastasia herself…A pleaser for fans of Michael Scott's Secrets of the Immortal Nicholas Flamel series."

—*Kirkus*

"This is a fun action story, moving quickly and easily through adventures and magic…which helps reluctant readers."

—*Library Media Connection*

"The intricate, well-paced plot…feels plenty original, and kids will be charmed by [Kirov's] brand of magic."

—*Publishers Weekly*

"Exotic locale, unusual characters, weird food, polar bears, tigers, magic, and a thirteen-year-old boy suddenly discovering he is part of a Russian magical dynasty. Yes, fans of fantasy and history will be pleased with this new series by Erica Kirov…"

—*School Library Journal* blog

"This book is so well thought through that I am beginning to think that Erica Kirov may actually be from a family of magicians. I have been bewitched and I can't wait for book two. A *vonderful* novel!"

—*Children's Book Review*

"Incorporating famous figures from the past such as Rasputin and Houdini, this book is an exciting introduction to Nick's magical family and their quest to restore the magical elements that have been lost to them."

—*Young Adult Books Central*

"As the core of the adventure unfolds, the author seamlessly blends facts and folklore of Russian history and historical figures in the world of magic with her modern-day story."

—*Reading Tub*

"*Magickeepers: The Eternal Hourglass* is simply amazing. This is a story of great imagination, magic, and the power to believe in oneself. For lovers of Harry Potter, this new series by Erica Kirov is sure to be a huge hit."

—*Café of Dreams*

"I found it a delightful escape into imagination and intrigue."

—*Dolce Bellezza*

"Kids will love these books because they are fun and funny…and parents will love the fact that their kids are learning something (there's a lot of history from Tsarist Russia in this book). Parents will also appreciate the fact that their kids are reading and are enjoying it…If you know a young reader (anyone from about eight or nine on up, I would say), get them this book. But be prepared to get them the rest of the series, too, because they will be hooked."

—*Blogcritics*

MAGICKEEPERS

THE CHALICE OF IMMORTALITY

BOOK THREE

MAGICKEEPERS

THE CHALICE OF IMMORTALITY
BOOK THREE

ERICA KIROV

Magic is more than an illusion.

sourcebooks
jabberwocky

Copyright © 2011 by Erica Kirov
Cover and internal design © 2011 by Sourcebooks, Inc.
Cover illustration © Eric L. Williams

Sourcebooks and the colophon are registered trademarks of Sourcebooks, Inc.

Published by Sourcebooks Jabberwocky, an imprint of Sourcebooks, Inc.
P.O. Box 4410, Naperville, Illinois 60567-4410
(630) 961-3900
Fax: (630) 961-2168
www.jabberwockykids.com

Library of Congress Cataloging-in-Publication data is on file with the publisher.

Source of Production: Versa Press, East Peoria, Illinois, USA.
Date of Production: March 2011
Run Number: 14865

Printed and bound in the United States of America.
VP 10 9 8 7 6 5 4 3 2 1

To my children.

And to the memory of Fanny, who I never fully understood,
but whose life in Russia inspired this series.

ACKNOWLEDGMENTS

As always, to my agent, Jay Poynor, and to the extraordinary-in-every-way team at Jabberwocky. From the creation of the covers to the support for authors, they make it all a wonderful experience.

To the many kids who have taken the time to write to me—when an author feels like she can't keep up with her fan emails, that's a great thing. You have all been so incredible.

To the teachers and librarians across the country who have supported the series.

Finally, to all the kids in my real life—including the cousins, Pano, Eva, Sofia, Tyler, Zachary, Cassidy, and Tori. To my friend Jacob Phillips, who will always be special to me because he makes me feel like a real author. And to my breath and my life, Alexa, Nicholas, Isabella, and the Mighty Jack-Jack (future pirate extraordinaire)…you are the reason for everything.

There was something awesome in the thought of the solitary mortal standing by the open window and summoning in from the gloom outside the spirits of the nether world.
—Sir Arthur Conan Doyle

God has seen your tears and heard your prayers. Fear not, the child will not die.
—Grigori Rasputin

I have Immortal longings in me.
—William Shakespeare

It was on a bitterly cold and frosty morning, towards the end of the winter of '97, that I was awakened by a tugging at my shoulder. It was Holmes. The candle in his hand shone upon his eager, stooping face, and told me at a glance that something was amiss.
"Come, Watson, come!" he cried. "The game is afoot. Not a word! Into your clothes and come!"

—From "The Adventure of the Abbey Grange,"
by Sir Arthur Conan Doyle

CONTENTS

PROLOGUE

Undershaw Estate, Surrey, England, October 28, 1921

*H*ARRY HOUDINI MANEUVERED HIS SLEEK BLACK CAR down the long drive protected by rows of tall trees, their branches vibrant with the red and orange flames of fall leaves. The route led to the stately red brick mansion of Undershaw, near the village of Hindhead. Night fell quickly here, and the rattling leaves of the forest lent the estate an eerie feeling befitting the night's activities.

Houdini parked in the drive, stepped out of his vehicle, and admired the peaked roof and many windows of the mansion that overlooked the surrounding countryside. He knew his friend's home had fourteen bedrooms and perhaps as many fireplaces to guard against the chill. Houdini's boots crunched on the gravel as he walked to the imposing wooden door and rang the bell. A butler answered the door.

"I am here to see Sir Arthur Conan Doyle. I believe he is expecting me," said the world's most famous magician and escape artist, clutching his hat in his hand.

The butler offered a simple nod. "Indeed, Mr. Houdini, the others have all assembled. You may follow me, sir."

Houdini stepped into a great foyer with an enormous crystal chandelier that twinkled with shimmering light, following behind the butler, his footsteps echoing on the black and white marble floors. He passed suits of shining armor; swords crossed on the walls; and stuffed hunting trophies, including a large moose head, as well as a bear and a pheasant. Occasionally, a framed photo of the famous Sherlock Holmes author accepting one honor or another was displayed with prominence.

At the end of a long hall, Houdini was shown into a cavernous library.

"Mister Houdini, sir," the butler announced.

"Splendid!" Sir Arthur Conan Doyle chortled. He rose from his leather chair by the roaring fireplace and crossed the room with three strides of his long legs, handlebar mustache twitching. "Harry, my dear friend, how are you?"

"Excellent, Arthur, excellent. And you are well, I hope?"

"Somewhat. Somewhat..." Doyle's eyes darkened for a moment.

Houdini knew his friend had been plagued by depression

after the deaths of his brother and son. He had taken quite particularly hard the death of Kingsley, his oldest son, from pneumonia after serving in the war a couple of years previously. Houdini had often wondered if Doyle would ever recover and had worried that perhaps he might never return to his former self.

"I know, Arthur. I understand. After the death of my mother…well, you know how difficult it has been for me, as well. Grief…grief is a strange beast and an unwelcome companion, indeed."

"Tonight, perhaps, we shall speak with Kingsley—and with your mother. Let me introduce you to the rest of our guests." Doyle gestured with an outstretched arm. "You know my wife, Jean."

Houdini nodded to his friend's wife. "Yes, indeed. Hello, Jean. Good to see you again."

"And this here is a close family friend, Dr. Robert Shaw, who lives in Hindhead, not two miles away. We are also joined tonight by a dear friend from London, in for a fortnight's visit—Samuel Barker, a barrister and excellent storyteller, I might add."

Houdini greeted each gentleman with a small bow, but his gaze was mostly fixated on the woman in a high-backed, ornately carved wooden chair near Sir Arthur Conan Doyle.

"And of course, our guest of honor. Mr. Harry Houdini, may I present to you Madame Bogdanovich."

With a sweep of his hand, the author gestured toward the woman, who had elaborate velvet clothes and eyes made up like glittering butterflies. Her fingernails were lacquered a deep purple and as long as talons.

"The pleasure, Mr. Houdini, *eez* all mine." She spoke in a husky tone with a thick Russian accent and waved her hand slightly. Bracelets made of gold and encrusted with jewels—rubies, emeralds, amethysts, diamonds, and sapphires—clinked from her wrist to her elbow.

Doyle twirled the end of his mustache. "Madame Bogdanovich is a fortune teller and spiritualist of international renown. She has read for the crown princes of various nations and for the tsar and tsarina of Russia. Tonight, she has agreed to look into the unknown of the great spirit world to speak with our loved ones who have departed."

Houdini narrowed his gaze. He was used to fools who believed frauds and charlatans. People were often so impressed by his own magic tricks, illusions, and feats of escape that they believed he was capable of speaking to the dead or could perform real magic, with gifts granted from some unseen force. Since he knew his tricks were achieved through mortal means, he cast a suspicious eye toward so-called psychics. He was deeply concerned that his friend

Arthur was so easily taken in by wild claims of spiritualists. Grief had rendered his friend vulnerable.

"Pleased to meet you, Madame Bogdanovich." Houdini spoke in measured tones.

"You may call me Madame B."

"Excellent, Madame B. I shall be watching you very closely during this séance."

"Indeed you will. Your reputation precedes you, Mr. Houdini. You, sir, are a doubter of magic—even as you create your own illusions."

"Ah," Houdini replied, enjoying the debate, "but therein lies an important difference between you and me. In my case, I freely admit to all gathered here that I do, in fact, create illusions. No real magic is involved. I have no claims to contact the spirit world."

"Then we shall see," Madame B. purred, "if I cannot make a believer of you yet, sir. This *vill* be my greatest challenge!"

"You can try," Houdini replied.

"Come, let us gather around the table," Madame B. said. "Sir Arthur and Mr. Houdini shall be right next to me, at my left hand and right hand. That way," she batted her eyes—with their long, false lashes—at Houdini, "you may keep a close *vatch* over me, to see if, as they say, I have something up my sleeve."

The guests gathered around a mahogany table with elaborate claw-foot legs. Houdini took his assigned seat.

He immediately ran his hands beneath the table, feeling the wood for a false bottom or hidden lever. He touched his own chair and then carefully examined the chair in which Madame B. sat. He studied the room. Books lined shelves from floor to ceiling, but he saw no place for a coconspirator to hide. The room had no closet. He also did not believe that Arthur would intentionally deceive him. Therefore, he concentrated on Madame B.

Next to her chair, Madame B. had a large, black leather satchel nearly four feet high and three feet wide. She opened it and withdrew a candelabrum and a crystal ball on a pedestal. She placed them on the table. Houdini peered closely at them. The pedestal was gold, and all around its circular edges were hieroglyphics—Egyptian symbols. The pedestal alone had to be worth a fortune! The crystal ball was clear and flawless, without a single scratch to mar its surface.

"Please, Mrs. Doyle, would you light the candles?"

"Certainly," said Sir Arthur's wife. She rose from her chair and took a long match set from the fireplace mantle. She struck a match and carefully lit each of the white tapers.

"Now, if you would turn down your lamps. The spirit world, the world of magic, prefers the shadows."

Mrs. Doyle turned down the lamps until the room around the table was almost pitch black, with only the flickering candle flames for light.

The mood in the room grew both somber and expectant. Even Houdini, trying not to be swayed by the theatrics of Madame B., had to admit something electrifying was in the air.

"Let us join hands," Madame B. said.

Around the table, they all held hands. Houdini thought he felt a tingle of anticipation when Madame B. took his hand in hers, but he shook his head and fought to remain impartial. He was determined to expose her as a fraud preying upon his grieving friend.

"I call up the magic world, the world of wonders, the spirit world of my ancestors, the world of the Magickeepers, to speak to us. From the sands of time, speak to us. I ask that the magic world reveal secrets. These secrets will remove the doubters within our midst, will serve to show them that magic is real."

The room was deathly quiet—as quiet as a graveyard, Houdini mused.

"Breathe as one," Madame B. commanded. "In…out… together…united…in…out…"

Houdini heard Shaw, next to him, breathing in unison with Madame B. He glanced across the table. Doyle was a study in concentration. He breathed in…out…united with those next to him.

Then in the midst of the darkness of the study, illuminated

only by the flickering candles, Harry Houdini saw that the crystal ball was glowing.

Houdini's eyes widened as he stared at it. The ball was perhaps the size of a large grapefruit or a small melon. It sat on the gold pedestal with the hieroglyphics around it. The glowing ball grew brighter, and he heard Mrs. Doyle gasp.

"Remain calm," Madame B. intoned. "We must make the spirit world feel welcome."

Houdini stared. What sort of trickery was this? How was she performing this trick, especially when he and Arthur held both her hands?

"Ancient Magickeepers, speak to me. Speak through me. You know what answers we seek."

Madame B. shut her eyes. The ball filled with amber smoke and then with moving pictures. Harry would have rubbed his eyes was he not intent on holding firm to Madame B.

"It cannot be," he whispered. There inside the ball was a moving picture of himself when he was nine years old. He thought his heart might stop. He had never seen such a thing.

"Harry Houdini," Madame B. spoke, her voice dreamy, as if she were speaking from far away, calling to him from down a tunnel. "You called yourself the Prince of Air, performing on a trapeze as a young boy. Answer me! Was that so?"

"Yes! But surely this cannot be!"

Around the table, the other participants in the séance were transfixed. All of them stared intently at the little boy on the trapeze. He performed feat after feat, smiling, clearly reveling in his antics on the trapeze while trapped inside the crystal ball. He performed a flip off the trapeze and waved at an unseen person, beaming and grinning.

"There," Madame B. continued, "the Prince of Air waves at his mother, who has since departed this world."

Houdini's eyes filled with tears. He remembered that day, and he had indeed been waving at his mother, who had always been his biggest supporter, the person who cheered him on most heartily no matter what he did in life.

The smoke in the ball grew dark—almost oily—in appearance. Madame Bogdanovich's face paled. "Harry Houdini, mark my words this night: One day, you will come face to face with evil. You must be careful. On Halloween night, years from now, you will be paid a visit. You will know this visitor by his eyes. Fear him. Protect yourself. Or you will die."

Harry felt as if a spider had skittered up his spine. He nodded, throat dry.

The ball changed color again. Inside was another moving picture, this time of a young man. The ball glowed an incandescent greenish-blue.

"It is Kingsley," Doyle whispered, voice tremulous. He

looked at his wife, then at Madame B., then at the ball. "My son is moving his lips. What is he saying?"

"He says he is with *Touie*. Do you know this name?"

"That is his mother, my first wife. She passed away."

"This, he says, is the anniversary of his death. Is that so, Sir Arthur?"

Arthur nodded. "I did not tell you, but I...I thought perhaps his spirit might be strongest on this night."

"He says, 'Weep no more, Father.' He also says to beware of charlatans, to be careful where you place your trust, or your reputation will be ruined."

Sir Arthur Conan Doyle furrowed his brow. "What does that mean?"

"I can only say what the spirit world allows me to say," Madame B. responded. The ball flickered, its glow dying. Then suddenly, a magnificent goblet appeared in it. Now it was Madame B.'s turn to gasp.

"What is it?" Sir Arthur asked.

"Sir Arthur...beware. Beware, my friend. Beware. A goblet may come into your hands. Protect it at all costs, but fear it! Fear its hold on you!"

"But...I do not understand."

The ball grew dark, again filling with an oily substance before it went completely cold.

Madame B. exhaled loudly and bowed her head as if

asleep. She was silent for a full minute before lifting her head again and looking at the people around the table. "That is all for tonight, gentlemen and Mrs. Doyle. Perhaps we shall try again tomorrow evening. You may turn up the lamps again and extinguish the candles."

Doyle did as he was told. Then he implored Madame B. to tell him more. "I am puzzled by your visions."

The woman shook her head. "Magic, my dear Arthur—the magic I see in the ball—is an imprecise science. That is how you can tell a true Magickeeper from a fraud. I do not pretend to know all. I only tell you what I see. I know the goblet I saw is valuable—and powerful. But I do not know how it will come to cross your path."

Houdini turned to Madame B. "May I hold your crystal ball?"

"You may." She lifted the ball from the pedestal and handed it to him.

Houdini was surprised by its weight. He turned it over in his hands. It was perfectly spherical, without flaws—no cracks, no marks on its pristine, icy surface. There was no secret button, and when he peered inside it, he could see nothing. No moving pictures, no smoke, no light.

"You want to see the pedestal now, do you not?" she asked.

"Indeed, I do."

She handed him the gold pedestal. Again, he held it in his hands and turned it upside down, looking for some trick, some ability to create the illusion he had seen. But he could find none. He ran his fingers along the hieroglyphics.

"What do these mean, these figures?"

"Magic is as old as time. Those figures recognize that."

"What say you, Harry, old doubter?" Sir Arthur Conan Doyle boomed. "I saw my boy in that glass. I saw him clear as day."

Harry nodded, still puzzled. There had to be a trick. There was *always* a trick.

"I do not know what to say, Sir Arthur." He frowned. If Madame Bogdanovich had not relied on trickery, then the conclusion he arrived at was chilling. She had foretold his death. And she had warned his friend. Evil, he decided, might be closing in around him and Doyle. This concerned him. Illusions…those he understood. The work of unseen forces? Those were things he had no desire to do battle with.

SERGEI'S CIRCUS

N ick Rostov and his cousin Isabella sat at their tidy desks in class. Their distant cousin and teacher Theo peered down his nose at them. He pointed a finger, and their test papers glided through the air to settle on their desks with a near-silent *whoosh*.

"F's. Both of you. I do not understand why simple history is so difficult."

Nick sputtered, "*Simple* history? You want us to memorize complicated magic from ancient Egypt to today. What is that, like a thousand years of magic?"

Theo laughed as he pushed his horn-rimmed glasses up from the end of his nose. "More like five thousand years, which is a clear indication of why you have an F!"

"But it's not just that. You make us study a family tree

that's so confusing, it gives me a headache. It's more like a family bush, it has so many branches. And all those names! In the Russian alphabet with that crazy Cyrillic…"

Theo's mouth smirked at the corners. "Speaking of which, your Cyrillic handwriting exam was worse. Worse than an F!"

Isabella sighed, scratching at her ankles. Nick glanced at her. He was itching like crazy too. They both fidgeted in their seats.

"What is wrong with the two of you?"

Nick shrugged. "Bug bites?"

Isabella nodded. "Bedbugs?"

"Are you trying to hang noodle soup on my ears?" Theo accused.

Nick shook his head. He was only now getting used to the strange Russian expressions his cousins favored. "No. This is no noodle soup! We really have bug bites."

"I don't believe you. Enough of this. You fidget like sturgeon flopping on a shore. You are both dismissed for the day—dismissed like smelly fish. For homework, you can each write a five-page report, *in Cyrillic*, on why history is so important. One word less than five pages, and I will make Monday's paper ten pages." He snapped his fingers in the air.

Nick groaned, collected his notebook, and said, "Come on, Isabella."

Isabella motioned for her white Siberian tiger, Sascha, to follow her. The sleepy beast rose from beside Isabella's desk, yawned, scratched at her neck, then padded after the two cousins as they walked down the hallway of the top floor of the Winter Palace Hotel and Casino to Nick's room. When they got inside, Nick started scratching like mad. He walked to his crystal ball and yelled, "Sergei! Sergei! You appear right now!"

When Nick had first discovered he was from a long line of real magicians on his mother's side, he thought crystal balls, snow falling on the Las Vegas desert, evil Shadowkeepers, and tame Siberian tigers were tricks and mirrors. Now he knew that his family's magic and magical items were real— including his crystal ball.

Sergei's face appeared in the ball, his wild eyebrows bouncing up and down like dancing caterpillars as he spoke in his booming voice, "Nicholai! Nick, my man, Nicky-Nick-Nick, Nickster-the-Trickster…what can I do for you, my friend?"

"Look at me!" Nick rolled up his shirt sleeves, revealing arms covered with tiny red bites. "You didn't happen to accidentally *lose* some members of your flea circus the last time you were here, did you?"

"Hey!" Sergei shouted. "I'm telling you that the flea circus is the real deal. You put that circus on display in your lobby, and the tourists will go crazy. Little fleas on flying trapeze. It's killer, my Magickeeper main man. Killer!"

"But you said they were *tame*," Isabella whined. "They're not tame if they *escaped*." At that moment, she started scratching her neck.

As if on cue, Sascha began scratching and rolling on the carpet. The tiger let out a snarl that sounded more like a moan.

"We're miserable," Nick declared.

"You didn't tell Damian about this, did you?" Sergei lowered his voice.

"Not yet," Nick said, knowing Sergei was terrified of Damian's power. "But if you don't get rid of these fleas, and he finds so much as one flea…well, he'll turn you—"

"I know," Sergei said, "into a flea on a baboon's behind. In a hot South American jungle. Awful!"

"Yes," Nick said, scratching at his neck. "Come get your fleas!"

The crystal ball went dark. Two minutes later, Nick heard a knock from the inside of his elaborate wardrobe door.

"Come in, Sergei," he called out.

The door opened, and Sergei stepped in. He stood almost as wide as he was tall in traditional Russian folk costume and tall black boots polished to a sheen. He carried an enamel box coated with gold inlay.

"All right, Flying Karamazov Brothers, into this box

before I exile you to Siberia!" He lifted the lid of the box and winked at Nick, whispering, "Fleas hate the cold!"

Soon, little black specks flew through the air and landed in the box.

"All right. So the fleas didn't work out," Sergei said. "But have I got a deal for you."

Nick groaned. "Sergei! No! No more deals for your crazy magic animals."

"Not even for a platypus that plays chess?"

"No!" Nick shouted. "Sergei...you know Damian. If he catches you in here with your lunatic ideas—forget it!"

Sergei looked hurt. "Fine. I will take my fleas and go home. But I promise you, Nicky-Nick-Nick, that I will discover an animal act that even Damian will approve of."

With that, he shut the lid of his box, stepped back into the wardrobe, and disappeared.

"Do you think he's mad?" Isabella asked.

"A little. But he'll get over it." Nick leaned down and scratched at his ankle. "He'll get over it before we get over these bites. He really *is* lucky Damian wasn't here to turn him into a flea on a baboon's behind!"

"I better get going," Isabella said. "We have a *paper* due tomorrow." She sighed as she and Sascha left Nick's room.

Alone, Nick flopped on his bed. He hated writing papers. His favorite parts of school were sword-fighting lessons with

Boris (at first, he'd thought Boris was insane and creepy, but now he liked him) and anything having to do with real magic. But history and writing papers? He cringed.

Suddenly, he had a strange feeling. He sat up and stared at his crystal ball. The back of his neck tingled as if he were being stuck with tiny pins. In the ball, a fuzzy picture appeared.

Crystal-ball gazing was not an exact science—Theo sure loved to tell him that. It was easy to misinterpret the visions. A Gazer had to be pure of heart in order to understand the visions' meanings. Even then, it was easy to misinterpret what he saw.

Nick took several deep breaths. He tried to push away the stress of school and anything that might cloud the vision. He tried to ignore his flea bites. And there, in the crystal ball was Madame Bogdanovich—the woman his grandpa had taken him to meet on his thirteenth birthday.

She was staring deeply into a teacup, and she was talking to his mother, Tatyana, who had died when he was just a baby.

Nick leaned close to the ball to listen to their conversation.

"I *vish* I had something else to say, Tatyana. You are beautiful and magical. You are the most brilliant spell-caster of your generation, but a prophecy is a prophecy."

"It can be changed!"

"No," Madame B. said sadly. "You shall bear a child, and he will be the leader of the next generation."

"But that means he will be haunted by visions, targeted by Rasputin. Every day, the mantle of his responsibility will rest on his shoulders."

Madame B., the gifted fortune teller, nodded. "But sometimes, Tatyana, leaders are born. They may not want to be leaders, but history and circumstances make them so. Your baby will lead the Magickeepers into the next generation. The prophecy cannot be unwritten."

"At what cost?" Tatyana asked. Her green eyes flashed. "I want him to have a normal childhood. I don't want him to feel like he has to fulfill a prophecy. Let him be a child."

Madame B. shook her head. "He cannot escape what I see in these tea leaves."

"Then I will ask Theo to cast a spell of protection."

Madame Bogdanovich's eyes flashed again. "You ask too much."

"Then I will leave."

Nick squinted and pressed his ear close to the ball.

"Mom?" he whispered.

But the ball grew dark.

Nick stared at it. The ball seemed to defy him, cold and empty now. Taunting him. "What prophecy?" he said aloud. "What did my mother know?"

But he knew asking questions was futile.

Nick sank down on his bed. His grandfather had taken

him to meet Madame Bogdanovich on his birthday. She was the one who'd shown him that he was a Gazer. Nick furrowed his brow. What did she know about his mother? He began to think of a plan to find out.

Crystal ball or not, Nick was going to discover what Madame Bogdanovich knew about his destiny.

ROAD TRIP!

*H*EY, DAD!" NICK SAID THE NEXT DAY, PROPPING HIS elbows up on the counter. His dad and his grandfather ran a tour company that took the hotel guests to see all the sights in Las Vegas. His dad wasn't a Magickeeper, but he wanted Nick to learn everything he could about magic. It was the only way to keep him safe from the Shadowkeepers.

"Hey, Nick…Theo gave me a copy of your report card."

Nick rolled his eyes. "All right, so…it wasn't that great."

His dad laughed. "That's a little bit of an understatement."

"You know," Nick replied, "you're not giving me any credit for how *hard* school is."

"But you hated regular school too. And now—now you get to learn…" His dad looked around the hotel lobby to see if any tourists were nearby. Then he lowered his voice to a whisper, "*Magic.* So it seems to me you should be earning A's and B's."

His grandfather walked over to them, his round, Santa-sized belly nearly popping the buttons of his tour guide uniform. "If it isn't my favorite grandson!"

"I'm your *only* grandson." Nick smiled. His grandfather was seriously in need of some new jokes.

"I saw your report card…"

Nick shook his head. "Tell you what—next time I get my report card, why don't you just have Theo blow it up into a giant poster and hang it in the lobby?" He gestured toward the enormous posters that adorned the walls advertising their magic show. He and his Magickeeper family performed six days a week, with an extra matinee on Saturdays. They made elephants disappear and Siberian tigers turn into princesses. Nick himself rode his magnificent golden horse and leaped over tigers. But what the human audience didn't know was that his cousin Damian's feats, and all the magic the family performed, were *real.*

"That's a good idea," Grandpa teased, his handlebar mustache wriggling with laughter.

"Well…you know, my report card is actually sort of why I'm here."

"Oh?" his father asked.

"I feel like I just want a break. Tomorrow, there's no show.

And the three of us haven't done something all alone together in forever. I miss our old all-you-can-eat buffet days. And I am so sick of Russian food. If I have to so much as *look* at cod soup again, I might choke! No more *ukha!* I want a good, old-fashioned American cheeseburger. And fries!"

"What does Theo think of you leaving the Winter Palace for a day off?" his dad asked.

"You're my dad. Isn't it up to you, not him?"

"Well…sure, but it's about more than taking you somewhere for the day. It's about keeping you safe."

"You and Grandpa can keep me safe. And besides, I'm getting stronger in my magic every day—despite what my report card says. You should see me levitate. Please?"

"All right. Tomorrow, we'll go on a road trip. Junk food and maybe a round of miniature golf," his dad said, almost a little reluctantly.

"Great!"

☆　☆　☆

The next day, Isabella pouted when Nick said he was going with his dad and grandpa for an outing. The two of them stood in the lobby as crowds of tourists with cameras and suitcases and noisy children swarmed around them, taking photographs of the ceiling and furniture—all exact replicas of the Winter Palace in Russia, where the tsar and his family had lived long ago.

"What am *I* supposed to do?"

"What did you do before I came to live here?"

She kicked at the end of a beautiful and intricate carpet with her toe. "I don't know. I sort of can't remember before you came here."

"I promise when I get back, I'll sneak you in some cheese-burgers—and we'll play cards."

She looked up at him. "And French fries? And a *real* soda, not dark tea?"

He nodded.

"What about a pizza too?"

He looked at his cousin. She was shorter than he was, with freckles scattered across her nose and long brown hair. And she was skinny, with delicate hands and thin legs.

"I know I sound like my grandpa, but Isabella...*where* do you put it?" He had never met a girl who could eat as much pizza as she did.

She shrugged. "Just bring me the pizza, cousin!"

Nick winked at her. "Your wish is my command." He turned and walked to the front desk, where his father and grandfather waited—along with Theo.

"Hey," Nick said. "What's up?" He looked at Theo questioningly.

"I was just telling your father and grandfather that they must be alert for anything suspicious. Be careful—all three of you."

"We'll be fine," Nick said.

"I'd feel better if you brought Boris with you," Theo said. Boris was the family sword-fighting teacher—and bodyguard.

But Nick had a plan—and that plan didn't include Boris.

"I just wanted a day with my dad and grandpa. Okay?"

Theo pushed his glasses up from the tip of his nose. "Okay."

Grandpa glanced out through the glass doors to the circular entranceway to the hotel. "Gentlemen, I believe our carriage awaits! Let us go before it turns into a pumpkin."

"I think you mean an eggplant," Nick muttered.

He and his dad and grandpa walked out of the hotel to Grandpa's waiting car, which had been brought by the valet. Grandpa drove a purple Cadillac—a monstrous, gleaming, *purple* convertible Cadillac. Complete with fuzzy dice hanging from the rearview mirror.

Grandpa slid into the front seat, and Nick's dad sat in the passenger seat. Since the convertible top was down, Nick vaulted over the back door like it was a high-jump bar.

His grandpa looked over his shoulder at him. "You could have opened the door, kiddo."

"I know, but it's more fun to hop in."

"Well, men, let's blow this Popsicle stand!" Grandpa said

and floored the gas pedal. The Cadillac took off with a *vroom*, and soon they were cruising down the Las Vegas strip. Nick had never lived anywhere but Las Vegas. He felt like neon was in his blood. Neon and magic. He leaned on the door and stared at the streets teeming with people. Music, neon, and noise, laughter and squeals all mingled in a cacophony. Las Vegas was home.

Their first stop was miniature golf. Nick had to resist the urge to use magic to get a hole in one. That was something Theo had taught him: Magickeepers needed to honor their magic. It was to be used for real battles, for good—not for foolish things. If Nick took magic for granted, it could betray him. But Nick didn't have to worry about his score. In the end, Grandpa lost one of his golf balls by accidentally hitting it over a fence, and his dad stopped counting when he took eight shots at the spinning windmill.

After golf, the next stop was one of Las Vegas's world-famous, all-you-can-eat buffets. Grandpa parked the car, and the three of them walked inside.

"Now, remember my three golden rules for all-you-can-eat buffets," Grandpa said.

Nick grinned. "I know them by heart."

"And they are?" his dad asked.

"Number one," Nick said, holding up his index finger, "start with the expensive stuff. That means shrimp, lobster, oysters, and anything from a carving station. Number two, no soda. Don't use up perfectly good stomach space on carbonation. And number three, take your time, because we're not leaving until we get our money's worth."

Two and a half hours later, Nick could barely move. Grandpa was still eating chocolate mousse.

"This was a perfect day," Grandpa said.

Nick's dad nodded. "It was a good idea for us to get away from the hotel, even if it was just for a few hours."

"Hey, before we go back—can we do one more thing?" Nick asked.

"What?" his dad asked. "Because I can tell you that after this meal, a roller coaster is out."

"Nothing that goes upside down. No...I want to go to Madame Bogdanovich's Magical Curiosity Shoppe."

His grandfather put down his spoon. "But I thought you wanted a break from magic today."

"I do. A break from *studying*. A break from Theo. A break from Damian. A break from the hotel. But...I really liked Madame B., and that was where I first Gazed. And I remember her shop was filled with all kinds of neat stuff. So I just wanted to go."

Grandpa exchanged looks with Nick's dad.

"Please?" Nick added.

In the end, the two men agreed. Grandpa paid the bill,

and the three of them walked out to Grandpa's purple beast. They headed away from the lights of Las Vegas to the desert, where Madame B.'s shop rose out of the sand.

A SINKING FEELING

ustav!" Madame B. purred when Grandpa, Nick, and his dad walked into the shop. With her thick accent, she asked, "*Vy* did you not tell me you *vere* bringing the *leetle* prince to see me again?"

Grandpa spread out his palms. "I didn't even know it myself until an hour ago. Nick said he wanted to come visit you."

Madame B. stared meaningfully at Nick. "*Did* he now?"

"You were the first person to show me I could Gaze." Nick looked around her shop, which—like last time he had been there—was crammed with potions, books on magic, props, relics, wands, crystal balls, and even a corner gilded cage housing white pigeons that cooed softly.

Madame B.'s eyes were made up like butterflies, glittering with makeup and sparkles, right down to rhinestones on the ends of enormous false eyelashes. She narrowed her eyes at Nick suspiciously, giving the impression that the butterflies were landing near her nose. "Perhaps Nicholai and I should meet in private." She put up one finger. "For just a moment, Gustav."

With one black-velvet-glove-covered hand, she half-dragged Nick into the back room. She drew the thick curtains shut, leaving them in near-darkness, except for the soft purplish glow of a large crystal ball on a golden pedestal.

"*Vy* are you here?" she hissed softly. "I sense *eet*, Nicholai. You are here for a reason."

"I saw you in my crystal ball, Madame B. I saw you when I Gazed."

She squinted still more. "And?"

"You read tea leaves for my mother. I want you to read them for me." He crossed his arms across his chest determinedly.

"No. I shouldn't have read them for her. Leave the past to the past, Nicholai. You do not know *vhat* you are asking me to do."

"Past to the past?" Nick looked at her incredulously. "You *do* realize you are talking about a family that's re-created a Russian palace from over a hundred years ago. They live in the past. All of them. It's like they are frozen in time."

"*Ve* miss Mother Russia. But *ve* study the past as a way to understand the present, Nicholai. Surely, Theo has explained all that to you. Wait!" She looked at him sternly. "Theo has no idea you are here, does he?"

Nick shook his head. "No. But I saw what I saw. My mother…she wanted to take me away from a prophecy. From the family. I don't understand. She was pregnant in the crystal ball, with me. I want to know what it means."

"But you do not understand, child. You cannot escape destiny. Your mother tried to run from who you are. But… Show me your hand."

Nick held out his hand, which she took and held palm up. She pointed. "There."

He gazed down at his hand, but it looked like his hand— the same hand that he'd had his whole life. Nothing special.

Madame B. slapped his palm. "*Nyet!* Look the way you *Gaze!* My goodness, *Meester Smarty-Pants*, you don't know how to Gaze after all this time? Look with your heart."

Nick stared down into the palm of his hand. It looked like crisscrossing lines. *Like a hand.* Sometimes, he really felt like everyone in his life was crazy. He took a deep breath and shut his eyes. When he opened them again, his mouth dropped open. His palm—it was moving. At least, the lines were. They seemed to tremble and shift as he watched. In the center of his palm, a small star formed, and it throbbed. It felt warm—hot, even—to his touch.

"What?" He looked at Madame B. "What is that star?"

But then it seemed as if the earth shook. "Did you feel that?" he asked her.

She nodded, her eyes widening as if the butterflies took flight.

"Earthquake?" The two of them ran from the back room into the main shop. The floor shook again. Jars and books fell off shelves, crashing noisily around them. The birds flapped their wings frantically.

"What's going on?" Nick shouted.

Nick's grandpa grabbed his hand. "I don't like this, Kolya," he said, calling Nick by his Russian nickname. "I think we should all get in my car and get away from here while there's still time, Madame B."

Nick's dad shook his head. "No. In an earthquake, we should stand in the most secure part of the building." He looked around as they heard glass shattering and a far-off sound like the howling whistle of a train.

"*Thees* is no earthquake," Madame B. shouted above the din. "*Eet's them!*"

"Them?" Nick's dad asked.

"Them!" Nick shouted. "Shadowkeepers!"

Nick's legs felt like rubber bands as he struggled to get out of the magic shop. He held up his arms to shield himself from falling objects. Books struck him, and shards of glass from broken jars flew through the air.

Madame B. ran to the bird cage and released the doves. She grabbed a velvet bag.

"Come on!" Nick yelled. "There's no time!"

"I must take the ball. *Eet's* my best one, the tsarina's ball."

Nick's dad opened the door to the shop and nearly slipped down the stairs. When Nick, Grandpa, and Madame B. reached the door, the sky was blacker than black. A suffocating darkness enveloped Nick like a heavy blanket. He couldn't see anything.

Nick concentrated on calling up flames from his hands, if only to illuminate the darkness. No sooner did he send a spark shooting into the sky than it was extinguished.

The ground still rocked, wildly buckling beneath them. As Nick scrambled down the stairs, sand from the desert rose up in spiraling tornadoes, stinging his face and eyes. Then the earth shook so hard that they all fell to their hands and knees on the ground, unable to walk—unable to even crawl.

The sand beneath Nick fell away. He turned his head one last time, and glimpsed the lights in the shop flickering through squinted eyes. Then he watched as a giant sinkhole opened and swallowed the shop like a humongous whale swallowing krill. Effortlessly, the house disappeared, and Nick felt himself sliding down, down, down into the sinkhole, too.

All he felt was sand…and all he heard was deafening silence.

CHAPTER
4

A SPELL WITH JUST ONE CURE

ICK FELT HIMSELF SUFFOCATING. HE WANTED TO BREATHE, but sand filled his nostrils and his mouth. He felt himself being sucked deeper into the sinkhole. He couldn't walk. He couldn't crawl. Panic coursed through him. His heart pounded with terror. He couldn't move.

But I can fly.

At the thought, Nick called on his powers of levitation, which always felt like a swarm of bats in his stomach lifting him skyward. He sensed the sand shift as he inched slightly upward. As hard as he pulled himself to the surface, the sand seemed to want to carry him to a gritty grave. He concentrated, even as he thought he was blacking out from lack of oxygen, and in one final *swoosh*, he burst up from the sand and into the air.

The sky had lightened to its normal color. Nick spat out sand and wiped at his eyes with his shirt. He shivered in the desert night air and looked at the landscape. It was as if Madame Bogdanovich's Magical Curiosity Shoppe had never existed.

"Dad, Grandpa, Madame B.!" he screamed. This was his fault. He should not have come to Madame B.'s. He had underestimated the enemy. How many times had Theo warned him about that?

Nick dropped to his knees and began digging at the sand. He felt a hand grab his. Nick concentrated and pulled hard, using whatever Magickeeper strength he could summon. His grandpa's head appeared up through the sand. He spat. "Pull me out, Kolya!"

Nick pulled, levitating and tugging. His grandfather was a large man, and Nick sweat with the effort. Soon, Grandpa was free. They dug at the sand and found Madame B. They both pulled her hands, and slowly she emerged from the sand.

"*Eef* I *ever* get my hands on those Shadowkeepers, I shall cast a spell to turn them into *steenky* cod, and then I *vill* make them into *ukha!*" she vowed. "And feed them to *zee* tiger," she spat as if for good measure.

"My dad!" Nick shouted. "Where is he?"

Nick stared down at the sand, but there was no sign of his father.

"Help me!" Nick moaned.

"Use your powers," Madame B. urged. She put a hand on his shoulder as if to calm him. "Use your powers."

Nick closed his eyes. He saw nothing but darkness. But then, almost like being pulled by some magical rope, he felt his entire body propel forward until he was standing near a scrubby cactus.

"I think he's under here," Nick proclaimed.

Rather than dig, Nick cast a spell to move the sand in swirls of wind that spun the grains up into the sky. When he was done, there was his father, eyes shut, lying on the sand.

"Dad?" Nick kneeled down next to his father. He couldn't see his chest moving. "Dad! Wake up!" He clutched his father's shoulders and shook him. But his dad did not move.

"Grandpa! Is he...dead?" Nick felt a sob rising up from his throat, and he pushed it back down.

Grandpa pressed his fingers against the side of his father's neck. "He has a pulse. He's still alive."

"But he—he's a funny color. So pale."

"He's not dead," Madame B. whispered. "He's *vorse* than dead."

Nick shook his head. "What? What do you mean, he's worse than dead? What's worse than dead?"

She seemed sad. "*Eet's* a spell. Come, we must get him to Theo."

"Where's my car?" Grandpa asked. "We're stuck out here."

Madame B. still held on to her velvet satchel. She pulled out her crystal ball. "I *vill* call my friend Igor. He runs a taxi service."

She set her ball on the ground and spoke into it. "Igor?"

A bald head appeared—as round and smooth as the crystal ball itself. "Madame B.! Haven't heard from you in a long time! You look great."

She patted her head of Medusa-like curls. "Oh, I am a sandy mess, Igor."

"Madame B.!" Nick snapped. "Focus!"

"Ahh, yes, Igor. We need a taxi. Right now. To take us to Theo. *Eet's* an emergency. Step on it!"

"Be right there!"

The ball went dark, and Nick heard a sound like a jet plane. Cruising through the sky was a taxi. A flying cab, bright yellow, descended and parked precisely in front of where they knelt on the desert floor.

The driver's-side door opened, and an older man emerged. His bald head was shiny, and he had tattoos from his knuckles to his neck peeking through his collar and beneath the sleeves of his T-shirt. The tattoos were of stars and moons—and words in Cyrillic.

Igor stared down at Nick's dad. "This guy don't look too good, Madame B."

"Please," Nick begged. "Just help us get him in the cab,

and take us to the Winter Palace Hotel and Casino—as fast as you can."

Igor lifted Nick's dad like he was a piece of luggage and slid him into the back seat. Nick climbed in there with him.

"Aren't you coming, Madame B.?"

"Are you crazy, Nick? I have to fix my shop!"

"Fix your shop? There's nothing left!"

"You'll see. At my age, I still have a few spells up my sleeves." She hugged Grandpa. "Take care of the *leetle* prince."

Then she kissed Igor on both cheeks, leaving perfect crimson lipstick marks on each. "And you," she purred, "you can come back and see me. I cook you dinner."

With that, Igor and Grandpa got into the front seat, and the cab took off through the desert sky in a blur. Within five minutes, it seemed, they had landed on the roof of the hotel.

✿   ✿   ✿

"This is very bad, Kolya," Theo whispered. He had sent Grandpa to go get showered and cleaned up. Nick's dad was on a blanket on the floor of Theo's classroom and laboratory.

"I don't understand. Madame B. said this was worse than death."

Theo nodded. "If you believe that when you die, you go someplace else—someplace beautiful—then yes, this is worse than death. Because your father is neither alive nor dead. He is in an in-between state."

The room was so silent, Nick swore he could hear his heart breaking in two. "Can't you wake him up? Please, Theo?"

Theo shook his head. "This is a spell—one of the hardest to break. There are rare and sacred spells that are from the origins of our bloodline. We do not even whisper them. They are spells that are too powerful, too dangerous, and interfere with life or death."

Nick felt a crushing sensation in his chest, as if his ribs were going to squash his organs. "But Theo, the Grand Duchess once told me that your magic was even stronger than Damian's." The Grand Duchess was sort of like Nick's grandmother. She was ancient and wise, the daughter of a tsar, and all the Magickeepers revered and protected her. "You *have* to be able to make my father well again. Please, I'm begging you—*do* something! Anything!"

Theo shook his head sadly.

"No!" Nick's throat tightened. "No! No! No! Theo— somewhere in your book of spells, there has to be a cure for this. There has to be! They can't win!"

Nick collapsed onto his father's chest, hugging him. "I'm so sorry, Dad. I'm so, so sorry. This is all my fault!" He clutched at his father and buried his face by his dad's neck. Then he lifted his head and looked at Theo. "I didn't appreciate him.

I should have appreciated him more. I should have told him how much I loved him—that I understood how hard it must have been to be a single dad all these years. I should have told him I was sorry for being a terrible student."

Theo soothed, "He didn't care about your grades."

"Yes, he did."

Theo shook his head. "He cared because he wanted you to do well, but he loved you no matter what. And I know he was aware how much you loved him. He was, Kolya. He loved your mother, and he loved you, very, very much."

"I did this to him. This is all my fault."

Theo walked over to Nick and patted him on his back. "This is *not* your fault. You're upset—and rightfully so. You need to get some rest."

"It *is* my fault. I shouldn't have asked Grandpa and Dad to take me to Madame B.'s."

Theo spoke softly. "You couldn't have known this would happen."

"But I should have guessed. I should have expected they would find me. Don't you want to know why I went there? Why I felt like I *had* to go there?"

Theo stood upright, walked over to one of his massive books, and began turning pages. "I think I know."

"Theo..." Nick took a deep breath. "I saw something in my crystal ball. I had a vision. I should have asked you about it. But I was afraid. I was afraid you wouldn't tell me anything. My mother left the family…and when she did, she was already pregnant with me. And I saw Madame B. telling her she couldn't protect me from a *prophecy*. Theo…who is my real father? I have so many questions. I think I always have. About my mother. About my dad. That's why I went. I wanted to know what Madame B. saw in those tea leaves. I needed to know why the Shadowkeepers hate me so much. I never meant for this to happen."

He stared down at his dad and felt a tear tracing a path down his face.

Theo sighed. "Kolya, your parentage is in many ways not important. I could not love you more than if you were my own son. Damian, Isabella, Irina, the Grand Duchess—even crabby old Boris—we love you. You are one of us. When you came to us, I could see in your eyes that you considered your father a failure. But he was a magician without his muse: your mother. I consider him a very successful man. He is a great man, to be admired very much."

"Because the tour guide business is doing so well?" Nick asked. He held his father's hand, which was ice cold. He tried to will life back into his father.

"No. Because of *you*. A man could be wealthy beyond his imagination. He could be a powerful Magickeeper, like Damian. He could be world famous. But if he somehow is a failure at being a *parent*, then it amounts to nothing, because that is the only thing that matters. *Children*. You have been loved and loved fiercely, Kolya. If you found out right now that the man whose hand you hold is not your father by blood, would it change anything at all? It does not matter what Madame B. saw in the tea leaves. Do you understand that?"

Nick nodded and looked down at his dad. He remembered, in a kaleidoscope of images, birthdays and trips to the skate park, bad microwaveable dinners and video games together. And he remembered the stories—the way his dad would tell him stories about his mother, even though Nick couldn't really remember her much. His dad had told Nick that when they met she was very secretive about her past and her family, but he had won her over by making her laugh with his very bad jokes. After they had fallen in love, she told him a Russian expression: *Eslib kazhdiy raz koda ya dumayu o tebe padala by zvezda, to luna stalaby odinokoy*. Something about stars and the moon; that if a star fell every time she thought of his dad, the moon would become lonely. Nick thought it was hopelessly corny. But now he wished he had paid more attention to his stories.

"I know," Nick said. "Whatever was in the tea leaves wouldn't change anything." He squeezed his dad's hand. "Theo...he can't die. *Please*." His voice choked off, and he felt like a lemon was stuck in his throat. "I can't lose him, Theo. I can't."

"There is just one chance for this spell to be broken."

"Anything, Theo. What? Tell me. I would lay down my life for him. I would do anything. *Anything!*"

"The Chalice of Immortality is the one magic item that can save him."

"What's that?"

Theo waved his hand, and a crystal ball that glittered like a large opal floated through the air.

"Behold," Theo commanded. "The chalice!"

ROMEO, WHEREFORE ART THOU?

The Globe Theatre, London, England, 1601

William Shakespeare paced inside his office. He owned a stake in the Globe Theatre, and the famous playwright was determined to sell out all three thousand seats for the staging of *Romeo and Juliet*.

But what occurred on the stage each night in rehearsals never quite matched the vision inside his head of what his play should be. He was sure all playwrights felt this way. The disparity between his artistic vision and how the actors on the stage performed his play tormented him and ate away at his soul.

He sighed and sat down, tapping his temple, thinking... thinking. His head throbbed. How could he make the play be more alive, more passionate, more true to what he pictured in his own mind?

Knock-knock.

Shakespeare called out. "Enter!"

In strode his friend and partner, Cuthbert Burbage, along with a man Shakespeare did not recognize.

"My dear Will, may I introduce to you Fyodor, a potential investor from Russia."

Shakespeare stood, bowed, and nodded his head.

Fyodor, a tall, stalwart man with hair the color of ebony and pale eyes, spoke. "If you would be so kind, Cuthbert, to allow me a moment of the great playwright's time? I wish to make him a proposition. In private."

Cuthbert nodded, clicked his boot heels, and retreated from the room.

Shakespeare adjusted his doublet. He was not pleased that he would be kept from thinking of the best way to put on the performance. He found this Russian a tad impudent.

"I believe, dear sir, that I know what troubles you," said the Russian.

"How would you know I am troubled?"

"You would be surprised, William Shakespeare, at what I can discern in the hearts of mortal men. I can see by the expression on your face that you are, indeed, troubled—and surprised that I, a perfect stranger, can know what is in thy breast, hidden from the world."

"If you believe it is purely a monetary issue, then you would be incorrect."

"No," the Russian said, his smile as mysterious and cold as a serpent's. "You are troubled over the final scene—the one inside the tomb."

"Indeed!" Shakespeare practically leaped to the man. He was startled by the intuitive way this man could read his mind. "I want the audience to shed real tears."

"At the line, 'Poison, I see, hath been his timeless end...'" offered the Russian.

"Yes!" Shakespeare shivered. It was uncanny! That was the precise point in the play that had troubled him.

"But imagine," the man whispered, "if you could perform that scene with the real specter of death over the actors. If the deaths inside the tomb were so *real* as to fool every single person who sat in the theater. Imagine the crowd, *weeping* as one, in horror, in shock, believing with every bit of their souls the death of Romeo and Juliet."

"Yes," Shakespeare exhaled in awe of the Russian's perception. "That is my dream. I lie awake at night, unable to sleep, knowing the scene falls short of my own demanding expectations. I am unable to draw from the actors the depth of despair I want to see performed on the stage. It nearly drives me mad."

"I have just the secret for you, William Shakespeare."

The man reached into a leather satchel and pulled out a golden chalice etched with symbols and a large red ruby on its stem.

"Fine workmanship," Shakespeare breathed. "Such beauty. I do not believe I have ever seen such a beautiful goblet in my lifetime. I am afraid, however, my good man, that I do not understand how this magnificent chalice will improve my play."

"Behold the ancient symbols on the chalice. These inscriptions are a powerful spell. Drink of *wine* placed in this chalice, and enter a state between heaven and hell, life and death. Drink of *water* in this chalice, and be restored by a single drop."

He handed the chalice to Shakespeare. "Feel its heat."

And when Shakespeare took hold of the chalice, his fingers felt as if they were burning.

"Is this the work of the devil himself?" Shakespeare asked.

The Russian laughed. "Indeed not. Just the work of a magical goldsmith, born in the sands of ancient Egypt."

Shakespeare put the chalice down on his large wooden writing desk. He faced the Russian, suspicion in his eyes. "Why, my good man, are you so interested in my plays, and indeed, in my worries? Why are you giving me this fine chalice?"

"In return for a favor," the Russian replied with a deep bow. "I must travel back to my country, but the journey is fraught with dangers, and I might not make it to my homeland alive. I am in dire need of someone who understands the value of the chalice to keep it safely. One day, I hope to return for it."

"And if you do not?"

"Then it must be safeguarded forever. You, William Shakespeare, will become its guardian, in a long line of trusted guardians of its secrets."

The audience in the Globe Theatre, normally a loud bunch, was silent except for muffled sobs. The young actor portraying Juliet spoke. "What's here? a cup, closed in my true love's hand?/ Poison, I see, hath been his timeless end:/ O churl! drunk all, and left no friendly drop/ To help me after? I will kiss thy lips;/ Haply some poison yet doth hang on them,/ To make die with a restorative."

Romeo looked, for all the world, as if he were dead. Shakespeare, disguised as a common man, velvet hat pulled low to avoid recognition, listened around him as people cried, moved by the play. Emotions had risen and fallen like crashing waves. Never, in his history as a playwright, had he so *felt* an audience captured in the palm of his hand, hanging on every word of his play, every nuance of the actors' speech.

He smiled to himself. Never before had a performance at the Globe Theatre been so moving. The death scene of the young lovers in the tomb would transform theater forever, Shakespeare mused.

It was the chalice. The actor sipped wine from the chalice and was rendered a near-corpse, only to be revived at play's end each night. The chalice…the magnificent chalice had made Shakespeare's scene *real*.

TO THE ENDS OF THE EARTH

"W E *need* THAT CHALICE," SAID THEO AS THE BALL CLOUDED over. "It is the only chalice that can undo a Shadowkeepers' corpse spell. It's that powerful."

"That exact chalice?" Nick asked, still holding his dad's icy hand.

Theo nodded. "And this one is no different from other magical relics. It has changed hands through history, been lost and then found and then lost again."

"So where is it now?" Nick asked, knowing in the pit of his belly that he would not like the answer.

"The trail has been lost."

"So it can be anywhere in the whole wide world?"

"Yes. But as in all hunts, we begin at the beginning."

"England?"

Theo nodded.

Nick looked down at his dad. "Does he look worse to you?" His father's skin was almost translucent. Nick touched his dad's cheek. It was as cold as his hands. "He looks thinner somehow." Nick brushed at his father's hair, which still had desert sand in it. "How long do we have to find the chalice?"

"Not long. Days. He will remain suspended between life and death, growing thinner and thinner, until…"

"Couldn't a hospital help him?"

"No," said Theo ruefully. "In a hospital, doctors would search for a cure for something they know nothing about. No, I'll cast a spell to keep him comfortable, and we'll keep him up here on our floor. He needs a quiet room."

"Give him my room," Nick said. "It's filled with my mother's things. He'd like that—to be around her stuff."

"Fine. We'll find another place for you to stay. Maybe you can room with Boris."

Nick shook his head. "No! I'm going to England. I'm going to hunt for the chalice."

"Absolutely not!" Theo's eyes sparked angrily. "No. You will stay here, cousin."

"I can't. I can't stay here while you're searching for the only thing that will save my father. No, Theo."

"I forbid it. Damian will forbid it," Theo said, referring to his brother and the leader of the Magickeepers.

"I don't care. If you forbid it, then I'll just follow. You always tell me that I am better off *with* you than doing things on my own. What happened at Madame B.'s proves it. So here I am, Theo. I'm not ever going to do anything behind your back again. But I want to go with you."

"Me, too." Behind them, Isabella stood in the doorway. "Oh, Nick, I'm so sorry about your papa." She walked over to them in her pajamas, her white tiger padding beside her.

Sascha nosed Nick's father's hand. Then she licked his palm. Nick thought he heard the tiger whimper.

"Sascha is sad, Nick," Isabella said. "I am, too. And if you go to England, I'm going with you."

Theo stood up and began pacing, pointing at them both. "No, no, no! The two of you get this insane idea out of your minds. I command it!"

Isabella looked up at her older cousin. "You always told me that we were stronger together than any one of us could be apart."

"But I didn't mean—"

"You didn't mean *children*," Isabella said solemnly. "But we are as brave as any Magickeepers. Even Boris thinks so."

"I will have to think about this."

"Aren't we safer with *you* than being here?" Nick asked.

"I am going to cast a spell to make you silent, the two of you. Stop arguing with me before you give me a headache. Come, let's move your father."

Theo levitated Nick's dad, and his body floated down the hallway to Nick's room. As Theo led the way, all of his Russian relatives opened the doors to their rooms and stood, heads bowed in respect, as Nick, Theo, Isabella, and Nick's dad moved down the hall. Nick heard them murmuring, "*Sozhaleju, ochen zhal.*" They were telling him they were sorry for his situation as he passed.

When they reached Nick's room, Damian was already waiting. He helped them place Nick's father on the bed sheets, which were embroidered in gold with the family crest. Nick walked over to his dresser and picked up a silver hairbrush that had been his mother's. He returned and gently brushed his father's hair. Strands fell out, as if he were melting away from inside.

Nick looked up at Damian. His older cousin had a tendency to be really bossy, but not tonight.

"Kolya, you have my word," Damian said. "We will use all the powers of the entire clan in order to find the chalice."

"I want to go with Theo. To England."

He expected Damian to yell at him. He expected Damian to tell him no in his usual imperious way. Instead, his cousin wrapped an arm around Nick's shoulder. "Theo and I have never told you the story of our own father and how he was slain by Rasputin," he said, referring to their family's mortal enemy and leader of the Shadowkeepers. "We were little

boys—much younger than you are. But had we the opportunity, we would have chased him to the four corners of the
earth and beyond, to Sanctuary, to the far reaches of magic,
and we would have tried to avenge our father's death. And
nothing could have stopped us. Let me speak with Theo in
private. We will see."

BANGERS AND MASH

*I*F NICK HADN'T BEEN SEEKING THE CHALICE, HADN'T BEEN SO worried about his father, he would have been excited to be standing with Isabella, Boris, and Theo outside Lady Daphne's Sausage and Tea Shoppe in Stratford-upon-Avon, England. After long discussions, Damian and Theo had agreed to allow him—and Isabella—to go, on the condition that they travel with Boris and obey Theo at all times.

"This shop," Theo whispered, "is owned by a Magickeeper. Now, when we are inside, keep your voices low. Pretend we are tourists."

Nick looked at Boris, who stood about six-foot-six and wore an eye patch that covered an angry, starfish-shaped red and purple scar. "Sure. Boris looks like a tourist."

Theo waved his hands, and he spoke some Russian words.

In a flash, Boris was wearing jeans and a T-shirt that read *Bald is Beautiful*. A camera hung round his neck.

"That's so much better," Isabella said teasingly. "He doesn't stand out at all."

"Well, it's the best I can do for right now. Come along."

They walked into the sausage shop, a red brick building that looked as old as the lopsided side street on which it sat. A green awning hung over the picture window, which was filled with sausage and hanging meats. A little bell rang over the door.

Inside, Nick smelled meat and a hint of mint. He looked around the room at the assortment of small tables, where people sat eating scones and biscuits and drinking pots of tea. In the corner, a woman studied them. She had short, light brown hair and the weathered face of someone who had perhaps spent her life in the sun and wind. A long, white silk scarf wrapped around her neck. When she caught Nick staring at her, she glanced away.

"Is that Lady Daphne?" Nick asked Theo, nodding his head toward the woman in the white scarf. She certainly looked mysterious.

"No," Theo whispered. "Lady Daphne is over there." He jerked his head to indicate the woman behind the counter.

Lady Daphne stood very short and plump, with a large green apron on and snow-white curly hair. Her cheeks were ruddy, and she had bright, robin's-egg blue eyes. Nick thought

she looked like a kindergarten teacher or a grandmother—
except her apron was covered with blood and sausage bits.
She also carried a giant meat cleaver that Nick was certain
could chop his head off. Nick decided then and there that he
would not want to cross Lady Daphne and her sausages.

Theo said, "Sit down at that table over there. We'll order
some bangers and mash and wait until she can come to the
table to talk to us."

They all sat down at a round table with a green and white
checkered tablecloth. "Bangers and mash?" Nick asked.

Boris looked at the menu. "Bangers and mash are sausages
and mashed potatoes. We can get them with onion gravy.
I am very hungry."

Here Nick thought he had escaped Russian food—the
hideously salty caviar, cod soup (*ukha!*), borscht (what were
his ancestors thinking when they decided on blood-red soup
made of *beets?*). Now—bangers and mash for breakfast!

Nick shuddered slightly.

A short time later, Lady Daphne came over, wiping her
hands on her apron and streaking it with crimson stains.

"Well, call me gobsmacked. 'Ello, Theo!"

Theo smiled at her. "Lady Daphne, we're here *sightseeing*."
He winked at her. "I'd like it if you could bring us each
some bangers and mash. Your finest! And a pot of tea. Dark
Russian tea, if you have it."

"'Fraid you'll 'ave to settle for English breakfast tea. But the rest? You won't be sorry! Comin' right up." She smiled at him and winked. Then she walked behind the counter and into the kitchen. A short time later, she returned with plates of thick mashed potatoes piled with sausages and then slathered in dark brown-red gravy and onions. Nick was so hungry that he dug in, even though this was the least-appetizing breakfast he'd ever seen.

Lady Daphne pulled up a wooden chair and plopped into it. She was so short that her feet barely touched the ground when she was sitting in it. "I 'ear you seek the chalice," she whispered.

Theo nodded. "We do."

"The trail is cold, but I suggest starting at Henley Street in Shakespeare's boyhood home. Then see where it leads you. You'll have to go at night, after it's closed."

"Have you seen signs of the evil ones about?" Boris asked.

"I see shadows. After nightfall. Beware. For tonight, I have a bed and breakfast on the edge of town—a place that," she dropped her voice to a whisper, "caters to our kind. You may stay the night."

Later, near midnight, after the real tourists had gone, Theo, Boris, Isabella, and Nick stood in the silence of Shakespeare's boyhood home. They were invisible to any security cameras, shielded by one of Theo's spells. Isabella whispered, "It's creepy in here."

The windows were a thick, leaded glass that didn't allow any moonlight into the room—and though the moon was full, it was as dark as a coffin inside.

"Come on," Nick breathed. He walked through the rooms downstairs while Theo went up the creaking steps to the top floor. Each of them touched the walls, touched objects, hoping to feel some connection to the place where Shakespeare was born. Nick hoped for a clue to the chalice's whereabouts.

But he came up with nothing.

"I don't get it," he said to Isabella and Boris. "There's nothing here." He looked at the desk, at the chair, at framed objects on the wall. In the quiet, he heard the tick-tick-ticking of a clock.

"Then obviously," Isabella said, "he never brought the chalice here. This is his *boyhood* home. In the crystal ball, he was already grown. He must never have come back here with the chalice."

"A dead end. So now what?" Nick exhaled in frustration. "Do we go to every home he ever lived in? That will take too long." A vision popped in his head of his father lying on the bed, the spell's cold paleness rendering him a shadow of his former self.

Theo descended the staircase and stood with them. "I detect no clues here. Let's go to Lady Daphne's bed and breakfast."

Isabella shuddered. "I'm afraid she might turn me into a sausage."

Boris let out a loud guffaw. "A sausage?"

"Yes. Did you see that cleaver? She scares me. And all that blood on her hands! She might put me through a meat grinder!"

Boris continued laughing as they walked out the back door of the house and down quiet moonlit streets toward the bed and breakfast.

Lady Daphne's special bed and breakfast for Magickeepers was on the very edge of town. Illuminated by the moon, the inn had a thatched roof that made it look like it had been built in Shakespeare's time, Nick thought. Maybe it had. Unlike Las Vegas, everything in this part of England seemed *old*. Flowers surrounded the inn, growing in shades of purple and red and pink. The wind rustled the hedges. A full moon looked like a perfect white wafer cookie in the sky.

Nick was tired and frustrated. He just wanted to go to sleep and start looking for the chalice tomorrow.

And then he heard it.

The unmistakable mournful howl of a wolf echoing through the air.

HOWL AT THE MOON

A CHILLY BREEZE BLEW ACROSS NICK'S FOREHEAD, FEELING like icy fingertips. Isabella inhaled. Theo and Boris froze. From behind them, they heard the sound of many paws scraping on cobblestones.

Slowly, Nick turned around. "Theo?" he whispered.

His cousin spun slowly along with Boris and Isabella.

"This is not good," Theo said. "Not good at all."

An entire pack of wolves crept toward them, fur sticking up straight along the ridges of their spines. The wolves were panting, snarling, and saliva dripped to the street. The beasts emitted low growls from their throats.

"Now would be as good a time as any to make us disappear, Theo," Nick urged.

"But if we do that, we won't find out why they are here.

Isabella," Theo commanded, "speak to them. Explain that we mean no harm."

"There are seven of them," Isabella said, her teeth chattering, eyes wide. The animals snapped their teeth, and one of them howled again, sending a skittering shiver up Nick's back.

"So?" Nick asked. "Just talk to them. Come on, Isabella!"

"Seven *angry* wolves. And those two," Isabella nodded with her head, "are the alpha and his mate—they're the angriest of all!"

A wolf leaped toward them, and Boris leaned down to pull a dagger from a sheath strapped to his leg. The dagger gleamed. Boris and the wolf faced off against each other.

"Now would be the time to speak to them, Isabella," Theo urged.

Isabella nodded and began speaking. Nick had always marveled at his cousin's magical talent—a skill only inherited by female Magickeepers. She could understand any animal—whether it was a barking dog, a chattering monkey, or her tiger, Sascha. And when she spoke, they understood her. Nick once asked her how that worked, and she said she had no idea—just like he could not explain how it was that he Gazed.

His cousin's voice was shaky, a little above a whisper. "We mean you no harm. We are searching for an ancient chalice."

One of the wolves roared and howled. The others followed suit.

"What are they saying?" Nick asked.

"They say that they are not what they appear. They have been possessed by Shadowkeepers and commanded to make sure we do not succeed. They cannot control their ferocity. Oh, Nick, it's so sad."

His cousin's compassion for animals was limitless. Nick thought it gave her courage, because Isabella's voice steadied and grew louder. "You do not need to harm us. Let us pass. We come in peace. We are Magickeepers and fight the very ones who did this to you."

Suddenly, one wolf—not the alpha—broke from the pack. With its tail between its legs, it crawled forward, almost on its belly. It looked up at her with yellow-tinged eyes and made a sound as if it was wounded and in horrific pain. Isabella nodded at the various whimpers, snaps, growls, and barks.

"Yes," she said. "Yes…I understand." She glanced at Theo and then at Nick. "The chalice exists. But we are not the only ones hunting it."

"That figures," Nick muttered.

"But we now know something else the wolf has told me."

"What?" Nick asked.

"The chalice was once in the possession of Sir Arthur Conan Doyle."

"Who's that?" Nick asked.

"The man who invented the character of Sherlock Holmes," Theo said. "Isabella, can you free these wolves?"

"I doubt it," she said. "This is a Shadowkeeper spell. I've never tried to undo one of their animal spells."

Nick grabbed her hand. "Isabella—you love animals more than anyone in the world. You can free them. Evil is *not* stronger than good. Don't be afraid. You can do it."

"I...don't...know..." She bit her lip. Her eyes filled with tears.

Then Nick had an idea.

"I should have known a *girl* wouldn't be able to do it."

Isabella quickly pulled her hand from his, slugged him in the shoulder, and began to speak in what Nick could only describe as wolf-language. Periodically, Nick heard her speak Russian.

The wolves howled louder. Their voices seemed to bounce off the moon and echo back again, surrounding them. And still Isabella wove her spell. The snarling reached a fevered pitch, and Nick watched the wolves as they rose on their hind legs, snapping and pawing at the air. They seemed to be hurting. Their chests heaved and expanded, looking like they might explode.

Wolf by wolf, they fell to the ground with a dull thud, one right on top of the other in a heap. They looked dead—all seven of them. Then Nick smelled it—the unmistakable odor of Shadowkeepers. He had tried many times to think of a way to describe it: Egg salad sandwich left on a hot school bus for a week in the middle of June? Garbage dump mixed with dead skunk? But no matter how he tried to describe it, words could not capture the stench.

"Look!" Boris pointed. Seeping from the wolves, a black, oily substance filled the street, forming rivulets in the cobblestones.

"Don't let it touch you!" Theo commanded.

Theo, Isabella, Boris, and Nick backed away from the oil and watched for several minutes. Finally, the wolves stirred. They shivered and whimpered and then woke up as if they had been in a deep sleep. Nick watched as they began sniffing, rubbing noses, and licking each other's faces. They looked as tame as puppies.

"What's going on?" he asked Isabella.

She beamed at him. "They are free!" she announced.

"I knew you could do it," he said.

Isabella instinctively rolled her eyes. But then she quietly said to Nick, "Thanks for pushing me."

The alpha male, easily 180 pounds or so, Nick thought, walked to Isabella and licked her hand. She buried her fingers in the ruff of his neck. "I'm so glad. I am so glad." She knelt down and buried her face in the wolf's fur. The other six in the pack approached and surrounded her, licking her and nuzzling her. Nick was in awe. He could barely see the top of her head as the pack made her a part of their circle.

She spoke to them some more, then nodded. Finally, she stood with the wolves still surrounding her protectively.

"We need to follow the trail to Sir Arthur Conan Doyle and Harry Houdini."

"Harry Houdini?" Nick asked, shocked.

"They were friends once," Isabella said. "Until the Shadowkeepers—and the Chalice of Immortality—came between them."

HARRY HOUDINI, THE THIEF

*T*HE WOLVES TROTTED OFF, FREE FROM THEIR CURSE. NICK, Isabella, Theo, and Boris wearily entered the bed and breakfast owned by Lady Daphne. She descended the staircase in a flowered flannel nightgown, her snowy white hair set in curlers, cold cream on her face.

"Blimey! You all look as if you've seen a ghost."

"Not a ghost," Nick replied. "A pack of wolves."

Lady Daphne paled. "Wolves! Oh, my!"

"They were under a spell," Isabella offered.

"I was in the shower. I didn't hear a thing. You poor travelers! The beasts didn't harm you, did they now?"

"Thanks to Isabella," Theo said, putting his hand on Isabella's shoulder, "no. It could have been far, far worse."

"What about Shakespeare's home? Did you find any

clues?" Lady Daphne asked. She walked to a large desk, opened a drawer, and extracted a room key.

"No," said Isabella. "But the wolves offered us a clue. They said we must follow the trail to Sir Arthur Conan Doyle."

"And Harry Houdini," Nick added.

"Oh," said Lady Daphne. "That's a sad tale—at least, the part that I know."

"Can you tell us?" Nick asked.

"Over a spot of tea. And here." She handed Theo the key. "The four of you can have the two-room suite on the top floor. But first...tea to warm your tired bones and make you sleepy. Mine is a very special, magical tea. You will wake refreshed!"

Lady Daphne led them into the kitchen of the bed and breakfast. A long wooden table of knotted pine stood near an immense fireplace with a crackling fire, its flames licking large logs. Above the fire hung a bubbling cauldron. Nick tried to avoid staring. Was Lady Daphne a witch?

She caught him looking and seemed to read his mind. "No, I am not a witch, you little rascal. It is my world-famous English beef stew with suet dumplings."

"Suet? What's that?" Nick's stomach growled with hunger.

"Why, it's raw beef fat."

Nick's stomach flip-flopped.

"Or sometimes mutton fat. It's the *best* fat too, the hard fat surrounding the *kidneys*. My goodness, my mouth is watering just thinking about it."

Nick wanted to throw up! What was it about Magickeepers and really gross food? "So you make *dumplings*...out of *fat?*"

"One bite and you'll be a convert, lad. Now, sit down for tea."

Lady Daphne prepared the table with a dainty porcelain sugar bowl containing perfect cubes of sugar, a small pitcher of thick cream, and teacups painted with portraits of famous Magickeepers.

As she set cups in front of each of them, she began, "Now to be sure, I have no idea what Harry Houdini may have had to do with the chalice, or what Sir Arthur Conan Doyle might have done with the chalice, for that matter. But I can tell you about the fairies."

"Fairies?" Isabella said, exchanging a look with Nick that said, *Even for a Magickeeper, Lady Daphne is a bit crazy.*

"Yes. Fairies. Two little girls—Elsie and Frances—took photographs of fairies in their garden. Sir Arthur Conan Doyle was *absolutely* convinced that they were real. And Harry Houdini was absolutely convinced they were a hoax. Though Houdini and Doyle had been friends, they had a falling out. A real row, from what I've heard."

"Were the fairies real?" Nick asked.

Theo laughed.

"What?"

"Now you're going to tell me you believe in fairies? Little creatures with wings?" He playfully slammed his hand on the table and chortled.

Nick furrowed his brow. "Theo…since I came to live with you, I've seen tame polar bears in a swimming pool, Shadowkeepers disappearing into oil slicks, snow falling in the desert, and a sinkhole swallowing an entire building—and just now, I watched Isabella tame a pack of wild wolves. Fairies? Why not?"

"Well, ducky," Lady Daphne clucked, "the fairies were not real, I'm afraid. They were a hoax. But the falling out? That was real. Go to Surrey, the home of Sir Arthur Conan Doyle. Follow the chalice there."

They drank their tea, which Nick decided had the taste of honey…and oranges…and mint mixed with cream…and something magical that tickled his tongue. Then they went up to their suite. Isabella had the small bedroom, which was an explosion of tiny roses on wallpaper—even the ceiling had roses. Nick, Boris, and Theo took the larger bedroom, in which the theme appeared to be blue stripes.

Nick slept on a striped couch. Boris snored all night long. And it wasn't just snoring—it was a loud sound like a buzz saw that kept Nick up all night. He tried putting a pillow over his head. He even considered putting a pillow over

Boris's head, but he knew he'd be taking his life in his hands if he did. Finally, near dawn, Nick slept for what seemed like ten minutes.

But Lady Daphne's tea must have worked, because the next day, Nick wasn't even tired. By midmorning, he and his three companions stood on the lawn of Undershaw Estate.

"It's kind of sad-looking," Isabella said.

Nick nodded. The house had once been a hotel, but now it had fallen on hard times. The grasses surrounding it had grown long—they almost looked like wheat fields, and they rustled in the breeze.

Theo cast a spell, and they found themselves standing in what once had been a library. There was no furniture, but Nick saw the bookshelves climbing the walls and assumed they once had been filled with the books of Sir Arthur Conan Doyle.

He walked over to a musty shelf and started writing his name in the dust. Suddenly, his mind flashed.

"What is it, Nick?" Isabella asked.

He whispered, "I'm having a vision."

Undershaw Estate, Surrey, England, March 1, 1925
Sir Arthur Conan Doyle sat at his heavy wooden desk,

working on another of his Professor Challenger stories. He enjoyed the jack-of-all-trades professor character he had created. Professor Challenger was so different from his most famous character, Sherlock Holmes. Professor Challenger had a huge head—enormous! And he was bushy-headed, fierce-looking, like a beast! He roared when he talked, bellowing like a braying donkey. No, he was not as urbane as Sherlock Holmes, but Professor Challenger was fast becoming Sir Arthur Conan Doyle's favorite creation.

Doyle leaned back in his chair and twirled his handlebar mustache contentedly. He smiled to himself. He was pleased with his writing. He looked down at his manuscript, which he was working on in longhand, writing with his favorite fountain pen.

Periodically, he sipped from a golden chalice on his desk. One day, he had poured water into the chalice and drunk it. He had felt a near-explosion of ideas in his mind, some energizing effect. So he drank more water from it. And after he drank from it, he found he never tired. His mind bubbled with ideas.

He heard a knock on his study door. "Enter."

Harry Houdini strode into the room in black pants and a black coat, his wiry hair looking, as usual, like he had been hanging upside down during one of his escape tricks. "Arthur, I need to speak with you. Your houseman showed me in." Houdini's eyes traveled to the chalice.

"What is it you wish to speak to me about? More of your doubts and condemnation of spiritualism? More of your sneering obstinacy about the world of magic?"

"Friend…I do not condemn. I only wish to save you pain and sorrow—more sorrow than you already have. Spiritualism—it is not real. You place your hope in falsehoods."

"No. It is you who are wrong. I am hoping my Professor Challenger will help people to realize there is more to the world than meets the eye. The spirit world exists, Harry, my chap. It exists."

Harry Houdini looked at his friend sadly. "Tell me, do these beliefs have more to do with that chalice from which you drink or the loss of your son? Or the dreams and disappointments of a writer? Are you not the creator of Detective Sherlock Holmes? Can you not deduce in the way he did? Can you not use the powers of reason to see that you are mistaken?"

"I am perfectly reasonable."

"No, you are not. You sip from that chalice and slip further and further into the realm of spirits."

"You are talking stuff and nonsense."

"No!" Houdini's eyes darkened. "You forget—I was there that night."

"What night?"

"The one night when I came to believe in this spirit world

you are so taken with. We were warned about that chalice. You were warned. I was warned. Do you remember the words of Madame Bogdanovich?"

Now it was Doyle's turn to become irate. His cheeks flushed. "I know nothing of what you speak."

"She said, 'Beware, my friend. Beware. A goblet may come into your hands. Protect it at all costs, but fear it! Fear its hold on you!'"

"This chalice has no hold on me!"

"When was the last time you wrote without sipping from it? When?"

"I do not wish to say."

"I've done some investigating, Arthur. I know how you came to possess this chalice."

"The parties involved were sworn to secrecy."

"You forget, I know how to hypnotize people. Using this talent, I discovered that after that night, after that séance, you *sought* the chalice. You were so bent on connecting to the spirit world that you assumed the chalice in question would enable you to speak to your son. So you used all your wealth, all your connections to seek it. You even sketched a picture of the chalice from memory—from what you saw in Madame Bogdanovich's ball."

Doyle stood up. "I do not need to listen to this!"

Houdini strode toward his friend and put his hands on

each of his shoulders. "You do, Arthur. You bought that chalice from an heir of Robert Knox!"

Doyle looked around as if he thought someone might hear them. But no one was in the room except the two old friends. He broke away from Houdini's grip. "And what if I did?"

"Grave robbing? Grave robbing! To obtain this chalice? Robert Knox bought bodies from the scoundrels William Burke and William Hare. They stole that chalice from a grave where it was to have remained hidden away from the world. For good reason. That chalice has special powers. It has a hold on you, Arthur—an unnatural hold."

Sir Arthur Conan Doyle put his hands up to his ears, like a child who didn't want to listen to his mother's scolding. "No, I *need* the chalice. It helps me create! And sometimes, since I got hold of the chalice, I hear my son's voice late in the night, speaking to me."

"It is your grief doing that to you. The chalice is unnatural, Arthur. Trust me, old friend. Let go of it."

"I won't. I won't ever."

Houdini sighed. Dropping his head as if in defeat, he nodded. "At least I tried."

"Please, Harry. I have already lost so much in my life. Let us not argue, old friend. Let us not argue and instead take a meal together. Tonight, my cook has prepared a venison stew. Let us eat and talk of old times, memories of before—before these things that vexed us so."

"Fine," nodded Houdini.

Sir Arthur Conan Doyle patted his friend on the back. He left the chalice at his desk, and the two men retreated to the dining room.

☆　☆　☆

Later, in the dark, Houdini crept into the library and drew heavy curtains across the windows. Only then did he light a lamp, casting the room in a chilly gray glow. He looked at his friend's desk. No sign of the chalice. Where had Doyle put it?

Houdini began opening drawers, working as silently as possible. He crept, catlike, around the room. He even looked in the fireplace for the chalice, but he could not find it anywhere. "Oh, Arthur," he whispered. "I fear you have come under its spell."

Quietly, stealthily, he continued opening drawers. He had to find it. It was too important. He stared at the bookshelves. Walking closer, he noticed all the spines were perfectly aligned. His friend was nothing if not precise and orderly. But one book nudged out from all the rest.

Houdini walked closer to it. He smiled. It was one of the most successful Sherlock Holmes books, *The Hound of the Baskervilles*. It protruded from the shelf above his head. He had to stand on tiptoe to reach it. Houdini pulled the book down. Using his right hand, he felt the spot where the book had been. And there, behind the book, the chalice had been hidden.

Houdini took the chalice in his hand and marveled at the intricate symbols, none of which he could quite decipher. It felt hot to the touch, and even though he did not believe in spiritualism—not the charlatans he encountered as he traveled—this was different. In all his life, that strange night with Madame Bogdanovich was the one time he was convinced the spirit world, the magic world, had contacted the human one. And even he had to admit that the chalice seemed to emit some sort of power. Unlike his friend, he knew enough to fear it.

Sighing, he extinguished the lamp, retreated from the study, and walked to the front hallway. There, with one last mournful glance, he whispered, "Forgive me, old friend," and opened the front door, slipping out into the darkness— and taking the chalice with him.

THE HEARTS OF MEN

*T*HAT NIGHT AT LADY DAPHNE'S, THEO ATTEMPTED TO place a ball-to-ball call to Damian. Sergei's head popped into the crystal ball Theo was using—a round ball on a small pedestal with claw feet that actually walked.

"Cuz!" Sergei boomed. "I hear you're in England! So am I! I have a performing monkey act on the subway—um, the tube, as they call it here. The crowd loves it. I mean, who does not love a monkey, right? Except when they poop. But my monkeys are well trained. I have a no-poop guarantee during performances."

Isabella and Boris were both asleep, and Theo and Nick were sitting in a small carpeted parlor on the top floor, each in a chair with a small table between them on which stood the ball. The walking pedestal paced back and forth like a nervous dog.

"I should turn you into a monkey for giving Nick and Isabella fleas!" Theo said.

"You sound like your crabby brother, Damian. He says crazy things like that."

"Oh, do I now?" Damian's face crowded into the ball too.

"Hey!" Crazy Sergei yelled. "This is my call!"

"No, it's not!" Nick snapped. "We were trying to reach Damian."

"Well, who said it's not a party line?" Sergei asked.

"Sergei," Nick sighed in frustration, "call back later. We need to talk to Damian."

"All right. But if you are staying with Lady Daphne, I bet you're hungry. How can you eat suet? Suet dumplings? She is a crazy woman. I would worry that she puts some kind of…monkey meat in those sausages of hers. If you are hungry, you call me. I'll bring Chinese food."

With that, Sergei's head disappeared, and Nick and Theo were face to face with Damian, the world's most famous magician. Damian was always pressed and perfect. His show uniforms gleamed with whiteness and sequins under the house lights of the theater where they performed. He never had a hair out of place—and his long locks made women swoon. He was always freshly shaven. That was why Nick couldn't believe what he saw. His cousin Damian looked horrible, with deep, dark circles under his bloodshot eyes, which were anything but bright and clear.

"How's my dad?" Nick asked, feeling like his heart was in the back of his throat instead of in his chest.

"Not well, Kolya. Not well. He's grown thinner, and his breath's shallower. Any clues?"

"Some, brother," Theo replied. "But the trail is cold, and it takes time."

"Tell me what you know so far."

Nick and Theo repeated all that had happened since they left.

"Tsk, tsk," Damian said, shaking his head. "It sounds as if poor Sir Arthur Conan Doyle fell victim to the chalice. His attachment was too strong."

"So, now what?" Nick asked.

"Actually, I can research Harry Houdini from here, see if I can discover anything about the chalice after he left Undershaw. I will report back tomorrow."

"Thanks, Damian."

"And don't order Chinese food from Sergei. I hear his kitchen has cockroaches."

The ball filled with burgundy smoke, then went dark and cold.

"What did he mean about Sir Arthur Conan Doyle being too attached?" Nick asked.

"Remember when you first came to the Winter Palace and you learned you could Gaze?"

Nick nodded.

"Well, Kolya, when you first learn about your gift, the temptation is to use it all the time—to rely on it and not your own natural smarts. What if…you didn't make *any* decisions without first Gazing? In fact, what if you stopped deciding whether to eat borscht or fried pelmeni for lunch?"

Nick rolled his eyes. "Honestly? I wish I would be able to decide between pizza and cheeseburgers, not beet soup and fried dumplings with sour cream."

"Yes. Okay. But what *if* you could not decide until you asked your crystal ball?"

"I wouldn't get anything done, I suppose."

"Precisely. But with magic, an unnatural attachment can form between a person and an object. Sir Arthur Conan Doyle kept sipping from the magical chalice, believing, perhaps, that he got his inspiration and ideas from the chalice and not from his own mind. Or perhaps after a time, he realized the chalice's magical properties stopped his aging. Perhaps he thought the chalice would make him immortal, which would be even more tragic, because immortality is not the natural order of things. Either way, the chalice began to dominate his thoughts. To consume him."

"Could the chalice make someone immortal?"

"It was designed to mimic death, and then to heal with a single drop. But drinking from it every day would invest the person with an incredible energy and life vitality. Drink from it every day, and yes, you could be immortal. But you would also be a prisoner to its power."

"Do you think Harry Houdini took it because he wanted to be immortal, too?"

"No. Harry Houdini, I believe, knew the dangers of the chalice. The temptations. Humans are such foolish creatures. Houdini knew, and he wanted to save Doyle from the chalice. He wanted to save Doyle from himself."

"Let's hope we can find it in time to save my father…" Thinking about his dad made Nick wonder about his mother, Tatyana. "Tell me about my mother. Before she left the family. When you knew her."

Theo's face took on a wistful quality. He leaned back in his chair and smiled. "Well, as a little girl, she was as stubborn as Isabella. She used to insist on trying to do everything Damian and I did. If Damian flew from rooftop to rooftop, she would, too."

"Isabella said she didn't have the animal arts gift. Right? What were her gifts?"

"Your mother was from the other side of our family tree. Her gift was as a spell-caster. She apprenticed with Madame B.—learned how to mix potions and to cast very powerful spells in the most ancient of languages. But I am sure Madame B. never told you that."

Nick shook his head, in shock. "Not once. Why wouldn't she tell me?"

"Sometimes," Theo said, "people believe children are best shielded from the pain of existence. But pain is part of life. It is part of death. It is part of the world of magic and shadows."

"So what? Did my mom use all that weird stuff Madame B. uses? Whale's milk and bat wings and tree frog saliva and all the crazy stuff in her jars?"

Theo nodded. "But she was more than Madame B. She… you know what intuition is, right?"

"Yeah. When you feel something in your gut."

"Yes. She had this amazing ability to listen to someone, to study them, and then know precisely what spell to cast, how to help them, how to nurture them. She could look at some of Madame B.'s ingredients and know how to combine them in some new way. She *invented* new spells—something almost unheard of, since we have so many ancient ones to draw from. She had power deep down that probably only rivaled Damian."

"What about you? The Grand Duchess told me you were more powerful than Damian once. Still are."

Theo's eyes stared off, as if he went far away. "Maybe," he whispered. "But—we all make choices. My choices are for the clan." He looked back at Nick. "I loved your mother—the way she laughed. She didn't laugh like anyone in the whole world. Her laugh was deep and loud and came from inside her heart. And no matter who you were—even Damian on his most impatient day—you would just stop and laugh with her. She had that effect on people."

"I wish I remembered her better," Nick said. "I feel like every memory I have is from Gazing—not a real memory." He stared at Theo. "If you had the Chalice of Immortality then...could it have saved her?"

"Maybe."

"Would you have used it to save her?"

"Not after she was gone. Once someone goes to death, they cross a barrier that should not be recrossed, Nicholai. Your father is in an in-between state, which is a different case. And had I reached your mother *before* she died, I would have done *anything* to save her. But perhaps—perhaps it's...better I never find out what I would be capable of. Immortality goes against nature, Kolya. It is precisely why Rasputin, our enemy, is as evil as he is. He not only promised immortality to the tsarina, but he has been trying to seize immortality for himself."

Nick sighed. "If we find the chalice, how do you know that one of us won't try to become immortal?"

"A sip will restore your father to health, but after that,

we must hide the chalice. Yes, the temptation will be strong, but we must not give in to the Shadows. It is why we guard our hearts, Kolya—why we remain true." Theo studied him. "I see you thinking. Your mother was a great thinker."

Nick ran his hands through his hair. "I don't know. I'm just worried about my dad right now. And—if I could have saved my mother, I would have. Even if it meant messing with the Chalice of Immortality."

"Immortality means watching anyone you ever loved grow old and die while you never age."

The Grand Duchess had watched her entire family be executed when she was a girl. "Like the Grand Duchess."

"Somewhat. But for different reasons. Unfortunately, in the realm of magic and the realm of the mortal world, people are blinded. They are blinded by greed. Hatred. Skin color. By lies. By arrogance. And in our world, by magical relics."

Theo stood. "I'm going to go to bed. We'll resume our search tomorrow. Good-night, Kolya. That is enough thinking for one night."

Theo walked into the bedroom and shut the door, leaving him alone in the parlor. Nick couldn't stop thinking, though. He sat there for hours, pondering his mother and his father and the things that blind men's hearts.

HOME

*T*HE NEXT MORNING, AFTER A BREAKFAST OF BANGERS AND mash with the awful red onion gravy, Nick, Isabella, Boris, and Theo stared at a huge map of England. The map was as long and as wide as the bed it was spread out on, and because it was a Magickeepers map, arrows moved and roads faded and then reappeared as magical routes superimposed themselves over human roads and tourist attractions. Letters swam and reconfigured in Cyrillic. Occasionally, a person appeared in black ink, but moving. One woman in a babushka—a Russian head covering—waved at them.

Theo spoke to the map, explaining they were searching for an artifact—a chalice. But none of the arrows on the map pointed to anything in particular. The four travelers tried to decide where to search next. Suddenly, they heard a banging sound from inside one of the closets. The closet door opened, and Damian stepped out, patting his black cloak, which was covered with dust.

"This woman is a horrible housekeeper," he said as he coughed. "Albeit a wonderful sausage maker."

Nick's heart skipped two beats. "Damian! Is my father—?" He wanted to shut his ears, wasn't sure he wanted to hear the answer.

"He is still with us," Damian said solemnly. "Nevertheless, I'm here to bring you back home."

"Home?" Nick said. "But we haven't found the chalice yet."

"The trail, like so many trails, leads back to the desert."

Magickeepers had their origins, Nick knew, in ancient Egypt. It seemed like sand was a part of them. Sand was part of the Eternal Hourglass—now safely stored in the vault underground in their casino. Sand had been part of the Pyramid of Souls, with its chattering hieroglyphics. The first time he ever Gazed with Madame B., he saw ancient Magickeepers in Egypt beheading birds and then reattaching the heads—dangerous and powerful magic. As Grandpa used to say, one slip-up and…good-bye head full of brains.

"When you say *home*, do you mean *Egypt?* Or…?"

"I mean Las Vegas. The Las Vegas desert. *Our* home. The Winter Palace Hotel and Casino. Come, collect your things."

Our home. Nick liked the sound of that. He and his dad had lived like Las Vegas nomads, moving from hotel to hotel over the years. Now, he had a home. And a family. For real.

The four of them did as Damian told them and then went downstairs to say good-bye to Lady Daphne. However, the ground floor of the bed and breakfast was silent. All they found was a note pinned to the front desk: *Duckies, I've gone round to the sausage shop. Ring me if you need something.*

"We can't leave without saying a proper good-bye," said Isabella.

"I thought you were frightened she would put you in a meat grinder, buttercup," Boris snorted, mimicking the motions of someone grinding sausage. "Now you want to say good-bye to the lady."

"I don't worry about being turned into sausage now. She's actually rather nice."

The five of them walked over to the shop, which was bustling with people buying sausages and meat pies. Nick stared. A wolf lay across the mat near the back entrance. Other people probably thought it was a dog—or maybe even a wolf hybrid. It was one of the wolves from the night before. Nick elbowed Isabella, whose eyes widened. She walked over, knelt by the wolf, and whispered to it. The wolf licked her hand, then nodded. Nick wished he had that power. It was just so cool.

When she rejoined Nick, she said, "The wolf is grateful. He says that the Shadowkeeper who imprisoned them was seen on the streets of London. The news was brought by an eavesdropping fox."

"Was it Rasputin?" Nick asked. The evil monk still lived, and he was determined to destroy Nick and his family.

She nodded. "They are going to take turns guarding the shop now. They will ensure that Lady Daphne and her bed and breakfast are safe." She grinned. "The sausage treats are a bonus."

Nick smiled at the wolf but felt someone else studying him. He turned and saw the same woman as the other day with the long white scarf and the tanned face sitting at the same small table with a simple cup of tea. She stared at him intently, but her gaze didn't feel angry or even dangerous. Still—his head hurt, which sometimes happened when he Gazed or when he encountered Shadowkeepers. He couldn't decide if she was a Magickeeper or not. He was going to ask Damian but stopped. After all, it didn't matter. He was going home.

Lady Daphne waddled out from behind the counter, her green apron covered in sausage guts. "Well, I'll be a Mad Hatter!" She grinned. "If it isn't the one and only Damian."

He nodded. "And if it isn't the best sausage maker in the world."

"You look after this one," she said, pointing at Nick. "Her, too," she added, looking directly at Isabella. "They've been through a fright. Now," she smiled, "you come give your Aunt Daphne a kiss, duckies."

Nick glanced at Isabella. The thought of kissing and hugging the sausage lady with her messy apron...*ick*. But they walked to her, and each pecked her on the cheek. She grabbed each of them and gave them a bear hug. Nick looked at his shirt afterward. *This will have to go in the wash.* He flicked off bits of sausage.

Lady Daphne pressed something into his hand.

"What's this?" Nick asked. It was a silver ball on a chain. The ball had tiny holes in it.

"A ball of my magic tea," she whispered. "I make it from my own magic herbs that I grow in the back of the bed and breakfast. This will help. Give some to your father. It will sustain him a little longer until...until you find the chalice."

Nick's father looked dead.

If it was possible, his dad's skin had grown more translucent, as if Nick could see through it. His cheeks were sunken, seeming to cling to his skull. Gray circles formed beneath his eyes.

Nick touched his dad's arm. It felt like ice water was in there. He turned his dad's arm over and looked at the veins—the ones near his wrist. Instead of a bluish tinge, the veins were silver. Nick heard a choked-off sound rise in his throat, and he pushed it down. He had to be brave.

He walked over to his bedroom door and opened it. A samovar floated in with hot water. A teacup followed on a floating saucer with a silver spoon. Nick shut the door and watched as the samovar—an ornate Russian water boiler—landed on his dresser. The teacup positioned itself under the spigot, which turned and filled the cup with hot water.

Nick took the silver tea ball that Lady Daphne had given him. He held it up, and it dangled back and forth on its chain. He placed it in the cup. The silver spoon floated over and then began stirring. The water turned a soft pink color, almost the hue of cotton candy. Then it darkened and turned violet. Then it shifted to crimson and thickened a little, like half-done gelatin. Then finally, it changed to pure liquid again, transforming color one last time to jet black.

Nick brought the tea over to his father. He inhaled and prayed that Lady Daphne knew what she was doing. Gently, he cradled his father's head and brought the teaspoon to his mouth. His father's mouth opened with a small sigh, and Nick spooned a few drops of liquid onto his tongue. He returned the spoon to the teacup, then helped his father close his mouth. Nick massaged his dad's throat until he was certain he had swallowed the tea.

For an hour, Nick repeated the spoonfuls over and over until all the tea was gone.

Nick returned his father's head to the pillow. His father's cheeks gained a little pink hue. Nick thought he saw his dad's eyelids flutter.

He leaned down and whispered in his father's ear. "It's Kolya, Dad. And I am going to save you."

Nick walked over to his dresser. He had an old music box of his mother's that played "Dark Eyes," a Russian folk song. When he was a baby, his mother would hum it to him. He wound up the box and placed it on the nightstand close to his father's head. The music box played harp-like notes. As it played, Nick sang softly:

Ochi chornyye, ochi strastnyye,
Ochi zhguchiye i prekrasnyye.
Kak lyublyu ya vas, kak boyus' ya vas,
Znat' uvidel vas ya v nedobryi chas.

When the song was over, Nick wound the music box's key again and left it playing. He stood at the door to his room and looked at his dad one last time. He remembered once when he was little and first learning to skateboard, he fell, broke his arm, and got a concussion. After he got out of the hospital, the doctors told his dad to wake up Nick every hour to see if his pupils dilated to make sure he wasn't getting worse. All that night, every time Nick awoke, there was his dad, *never* leaving his side.

Theo was right. His father wasn't a failure. He was a wonderful man, and Nick couldn't wait for his dad to get better so he could tell him that. Swallowing hard, he whispered, "Good-night, Dad." Then he went down to Damian's library, where his cousin had promised to tell him all he had learned about the Chalice of Immortality.

BANANA RIPPLE ICE CREAM

*D*AMIAN'S LIBRARY WAS THE FIRST ROOM NICK HAD EVER seen when he first arrived at the Winter Palace. On the night of his thirteenth birthday, which had been eight long months ago, his cousin had kidnapped him from his tiny little bedroom at the rundown Pendragon Hotel and Casino and brought him here. Since then, life had never been the same. Before he came to live with his Magickeeper family, he skateboarded, ate junk food, and tried to decipher algebra. He knew the world wasn't always a good place or a safe place—you only had to look at the news or the Internet to know that. But it was just the regular old world.

When his cousin brought Nick to the library that night, he showed him magic. *Real* magic. The snow that perpetually fell on the Winter Palace Hotel and Casino—in the desert—was real snow, not from a snow machine. His cousin really levitated. Crystal balls really filled with images and spoke from the magical realm.

But learning real magic came with a price. There were Shadowkeepers, and they had black hearts and hideous souls. The battle lines for good and evil were more real in the magic world than even what he had seen in his old life.

Damian's library stood at least two stories tall, and it contained books as old as magic itself—books written on papyrus, and even carved stone tablets. Some books were written with invisible ink. Some were in ancient magic languages. There were blank books that Damian would breathe on to make letters form—like the Magickeepers map. Some books talked. And every single book was on magic.

Way up high, the ceiling moved—clouds gently floated along in a mural as if blown by a breeze. It looked like a real sky up there. This was Damian's private sanctuary. Like Theo, Nick knew Damian spent his free time studying the ancient arts. He was the world's greatest magician. He was famous in the real world, but he was even more revered in the magical one. Magickeeper clans and families from around the globe acknowledged him as one of the leaders of the magical realm.

Nick found his cousin sitting with Boris, Isabella, and Theo at a wooden table. They were eating ice cream out of large bowls, and a five-gallon container with a big scoop was in the center of the table.

"Want some?" Damian asked.

Nick felt a spark of anger in his stomach. His father was dying, and they were eating ice cream? Ice cream?

Damian held up his hands. "Those eyes always tell me what you are thinking. You must learn to guard them better if you are ever to defeat the Shadowkeepers. Do not be mad, Kolya. The ice cream is a clue. Have a bowl."

Considering that most of the time, he barely tolerated the food his family served, Nick's mouth watered.

"What kind?"

"Banana ripple."

"Figures. You finally serve ice cream, and it can't be chocolate? Or chocolate chip? Or even vanilla? It has to be banana ripple?" Nick laughed despite himself. Banana ripple would probably be the *last* flavor he would choose, unless, of course, knowing his family, they invented caviar ice cream. Or beet-flavored ice cream. Or cod-flavored ice cream.

"This ice cream is a clue."

"You said that already. A clue, huh?" Nick raised one eyebrow. "This I have to hear."

Isabella looked up, whipped cream forming a mustache above her lip. "No, the banana ripple. *That's* the clue."

Nick scooped four rounded mounds from the giant

container of ice cream into a bowl that had the family crest on it. He grabbed a spoon and sat down. "All right. *Banana ripple*...how does it lead to the chalice?"

"Better to see for yourself," Damian said. He waved his hand, and a giant crystal ball floated over and hung in the air. Nick saw sand swirling inside it. Then Nick dug into the ice cream as he watched the sand settle to the bottom of the ball, and a strange man came into view.

The Desert Inn, Las Vegas, February 1, 1970
Reclusive billionaire Howard Hughes sat in a giant king-sized bed, sheets messy, watching the movie *Ice Station Zebra* for the hundredth time. The movie ran on an endless loop from a projector to a blank wall, and no one knew why Howard Hughes liked it so much.

The famous man hadn't left his bed in days. He hadn't left his hotel suite, on the top floor of the Desert Inn, in *years*. In fact, he *bought* the hotel just so he could live as he wished.

The room was dark and dirty. It smelled. Hughes had made one of his assistants tape all the curtains closed. In this dark cocoon, silent save for the movie, the once-great genius had descended even further into madness.

Hughes, a world-famous aviator, film producer, and

industrialist, was wealthy beyond anyone's wildest imagination. But he was now a mere shadow of his former handsome self. On the dresser stood a framed picture of him next to his favorite plane, the *Spruce Goose*. Made of birch, the plane was a beauty, with a wingspan over 320 feet across. The Howard Hughes in the picture smiled, his dark hair falling across his forehead slightly. He had a trim mustache, in the style of the day. He wore a dark fedora, with the brim at a jaunty angle, and an aviator jacket. One hand was on the wing of the *Spruce Goose*. His eyes sparkled.

That Howard Hughes, the man who had courted starlets and beautiful women, the man who had made movies and cut such a dashing figure was no more. Now, Hughes only cut his hair and nails once a year—maybe less. His long, gangly frame had wasted away until he resembled a living corpse, ribs protruding, skin like crepe paper. His graying hair straggled down to his belly, unwashed and greasy. His nails were six inches long and curled around. He was terrified of germs—ironic since he lived in squalor—and rolls of paper towels were scattered on the floor so he could use them if he touched anything.

Hughes heard a knock on the door but said nothing, staring instead at the flickering movie, mouth agape.

After several minutes and no answer, one of his financial advisors entered, an impeccably dressed man in a crisp, freshly dry-cleaned black suit and black tie, with perfectly clipped hair and a pristine, starched white shirt. "Mr. Hughes, sir, would you like some banana ripple ice cream? I can have the kitchen bring some up."

Hughes did not respond. He didn't even blink.

"Sir? We know how much you like banana ripple, but the flavor is being discontinued."

Still, Hughes did not respond.

"We were concerned. Very concerned. We felt like we had to act in your best interests."

Still, Hughes remained catatonic.

"So we contacted the manufacturer, sir. We asked them the minimum order we could place for your favorite ice cream to ensure you had a supply. We've had 200 gallons shipped here! We thought you would be very pleased, sir. You can have banana ripple whenever you want."

Hughes moved his lips, but no sound came out. His eyes were utterly vacant.

"Sir?" The man leaned closer.

"I..."

"Yes, sir?"

"I..."

Each word was more like a breath, an utterance, an exhaling.

"I..."

"Yes?"

"I…now hate…banana ripple."

The man in the tailored black suit frowned. His mouth formed a circle. "Oh."

Hughes continued staring at the movie.

When it became apparent that Howard Hughes would say no more on the matter of the 200 gallons of banana ripple ice cream that the man and his team of assistants had worked so frantically to secure, the financial advisor said, "Then we shall give out free banana ripple to all the guests of the Desert Inn." He turned to leave, muttering, "Of course, it will take us ten years to give it all away."

He exited the room. When he was gone, Howard Hughes's head lolled to one side. He no longer stared at the screen.

Instead, he started at a golden chalice on his dresser. It stood, alone, like a silent sentinel. Stretching his hand toward it, Howard Hughes breathed one word: "Immortality!"

LIBERACE'S GARAGE SALE

"So Howard Hughes ended up with the chalice?" Nick asked as he ate banana ripple ice cream—which he had to admit was not that bad. "Is what happened to him what would have happened to Sir Arthur Conan Doyle?"

Isabella added, "It's so sad." She put the rest of her ice cream down on the floor, and Sascha lazily licked the bowl.

Damian spooned some ice cream into his mouth, swallowed, and said, "Yes. Eventually. Magickeepers' relics must avoid human hands. Even in our care, they are dangerous. But in regular human hands, it is far too easy for people to succumb to madness. History is full of such tragic tales."

Theo, at the word *history*, held up his hand as he counted off examples. "Joan of Arc, Pythagoras…"

"The guy from math? That Pythagoras?"

"Wait," Theo teased, "you actually remember something from math class?"

"Yes," Nick said. "Sometimes, I pay attention, you know."

Theo nodded. "Yes, that Pythagoras. He was terrified of beans."

"Magic beans?"

"No. Ordinary beans. He held onto an artifact for too long. It manifested into an obsession with…beans! Anyway, it was good that Harry Houdini took the chalice when he did, or we would have heard some sad tale of what became of Sir Arthur Conan Doyle."

"Maybe he would have been afraid of brussels sprouts," Nick joked, thinking of his least favorite vegetable.

"So what became of the chalice after Howard Hughes had it?" Isabella asked.

"We're not sure. He was the temporary owner," said Damian. "Like all our relics, it seems they pass from hand to hand. Sometimes, they are hunted—like Sir Arthur Conan Doyle pursued the chalice from the grave robbers' heirs. And sometimes, I like to think the relics change hands purpose-fully, as if they wish us to play an old-fashioned game of hide and seek."

"So do you think it's still here somewhere? In Las Vegas?"

Damian nodded. "I do. I have studied every clue I can, conjured conversations with Magickeepers from across the globe. I've asked Madame B. to use her skills. The trail turns cold here. So this is where we will search. I feel it in my soul. I've called a family meeting for an hour from now. We're going to— every last one of us—search for the chalice. Those who work in the hotel will remain here for our guests, but the performers will go in search. We're canceling the show through the end of the week."

"What?" Nick's mouth dropped open. In the history of the show, it had never been canceled. Damian was a *legend*. He was the most famous magician in the entire world. He was on television. The president was a fan! The show was sold out years in advance. Damian *never* canceled a show. Not even when Nick's mother died.

Damian looked him in the eyes. "This is your father, Kolya. We will do what it takes."

The news that the show at the Winter Palace Hotel and Casino was canceled due to its star "having the flu" made headlines in Las Vegas. It also meant the entire performing family could search for the chalice. Many of them had never left the premises of the casino, and though the reason behind the hunt for the chalice was sad, Nick felt their excitement as they stood in the theater listening to Damian.

Damian paced on the barren stage, houselights up. "The rules are, you dress like tourists."

Nick smirked. Even Damian—who seemed very fond of his shining black boots, long black velvet cape, and Russian folk costumes—was dressed like a tourist. He wore jeans and sneakers. Damian in sneakers, Nick decided, was one of the funniest things he'd ever seen.

"Use the cell phones I gave you—no crystal balls. You may *not* use magic in front of any other people. Try to act *normal*. I realize that is…a tall order." He looked over at one of the sword-swallowers, who had a habit of sword-swallowing at the breakfast table. "I've given you each money. I've assigned you different places to look. Museums. Hotels. Travel by *cab*."

Damian looked at Nick. "And remember, this search is for Kolya. He was lost to us for many years, and now he has been found. We must do this for him, to right the wrongs done to his mother…and now to his father. Be tireless. Be fearless. *Oberezhnyj scheet predkov hranit menia*."

Damian's words were a spell of protection based on the circle of family. He repeated them three times, as was the way.

"*Oberezhnyj scheet predkov hranit menia. Oberezhnyj scheet predkov hranit menia.*"

"All of you, repeat the words as one," he commanded. The theater rang out, voices together. "*Oberezhnyj scheet predkov hranit menia*," they repeated.

Damian walked to Nick. He pulled a baseball cap out of his back pocket and put it on his own head. "I can't be seen out in public if I have the flu." He pulled the brim low.

"I think I need to take a picture of you in jeans, sneakers, and a baseball cap."

"No pictures. It's bad enough I have to wear these peasant clothes. They make me itch." He shook his head. "Come. Let us go." Then he, Nick, and Isabella walked out of the theater, through the lobby, and to the curb outside the hotel.

A yellow cab pulled up—and there was the unmistakable Igor, his bald head shiny, tattooed from his knuckles to his neck, behind the wheel. They climbed in, and he winked at them.

"Where to, tourists?"

"The Liberace Foundation warehouse," Damian said. "And no magic. Drive like a normal cab driver."

"In this traffic? Come on! Just a little magic?"

"No."

"You won't be able to tell. I can just make all the lights turn green."

"No. Not taking any chances, Igor."

The bald-headed cabbie sighed. "All right. Have it your way."

The cab inched along in traffic.

"Nick…how is your father?" Igor asked.

"Not good." Nick sighed. "That's why we're out searching. We're looking for a relic."

Igor nodded. As the cab pressed on, Nick asked Damian, "So who was this Liberace guy?"

"A Vegas institution. His name is synonymous with this town—or at least, at one time, it was. He was a piano player, an entertainer," Damian said. "A showman. And that's sort of an understatement."

"Was he...you know...one of *us?*"

Damian laughed. "No. Not one of us. Though," he smiled, "when you see some of his artifacts, you might just wonder."

Eventually, Igor steered their cab to a massive warehouse, quiet and abandoned in the noonday sun.

"Liberace used to have a museum—in his memory. But it closed. Now there is talk of a traveling exhibit of his things. But inside this warehouse—" Damian smiled. "Well, rather like magic...you have to see it to believe it."

Damian spoke a spell over the warehouse door. Magically, the door opened, and they stepped inside the cavernous building. After his eyes adjusted to the dimness, Nick decided he had never seen so much glitz and glitter in his life. And he had lived all his life in Las Vegas. It was dizzying! Sequins, glitter balls, silver candelabra, mirrored pianos that were blinding! As they walked through the warehouse, he couldn't help but stare.

"*Look* at these costumes!" Isabella said.

Along one wall, behind a brass rail, hung costume after

costume, most with long feathered capes and sequins, some with headdresses and sparkling turbans.

"He played the *piano* in those costumes?" Nick asked. "They look like something a show girl might wear. Well, except...you know, show girls sometimes wear less clothes! But those feathers!"

The fluffy feathers were shades of turquoise, yellow, red, and purple. Some were iridescent and seemed almost alive, shimmering like the scales of coral-reef fish or the plumage of jungle parrots.

"Indeed. He was an interesting man who loved all of this lavishness and sparkle. And in 1954, he actually met Howard Hughes."

"So *that's* why we're searching here."

Damian nodded, and he strolled slowly through the warehouse, inspecting every single item and artifact. He cast spells, opening boxes and crates. "Yes. Throughout history, lives have intersected. We search for the connections, and eventually, we will find the chalice. *Someone* has it."

Nick looked at picture after picture on the walls of the warehouse. The flamboyant piano player certainly wore strange costumes, and he always had a wide smile on his face—his teeth looked like they were from a toothpaste commercial, practically sparkling.

"Was he ever sad? Or in a bad mood? I've never seen someone smile so much."

Damian shrugged. "Most people have a public face and a private one. Who knows what anyone is like in their most private moments? It is the blessed man, the blessed person, to have those two faces be the same."

"Was he a good piano player?" Nick asked.

"He was a performer. That's different."

"What do you mean?" Nick stared at the smiling man in the black and white picture on the wall.

"He could have played classical piano just the way that Chopin or Beethoven wanted it to be played. But instead, he would do things like stop and talk to the audience. Or tell jokes."

Nick stopped in front of one picture. "Damian, Isabella—look."

The picture was a color photograph of Liberace's master bedroom in his Las Vegas mansion. The ceiling was painted like the Sistine Chapel.

"Oh, my," Isabella said. "Can you imagine staring up at that ceiling while you tried to go to sleep? That bedroom would give me nightmares."

"No, no," Nick urged, putting his face inches from the glass. "You two, look at the clouds."

Damian and Isabella leaned closer. "So?"

"Now look at everything else in the picture."

The entire picture, blown up to nearly the size of a poster, was crisp and clear. The colors were a little overwhelming. The bedroom was an array of gold—it covered chairs and was inlaid into furniture. But the clouds were blurry.

"It almost looks like the clouds were"—Isabella pointed—"moving?"

"How can that be?" Nick wondered aloud.

"I know how," said Damian. "The clouds could be that way if the painter of my library and the painter of Liberace's bedroom were the same Magickeeper. He fancies himself a Michelangelo—I'd know his work anywhere. His name is Vadim, and if I get my hands on him, he will be worse than a flea on a baboon's behind. He will be a flea on a flea on a baboon's behind."

"But...the painter never should have done that. He shouldn't have painted magic on the ceiling—should he?" Isabella asked.

Damian sighed. "No, he shouldn't have. But anything is possible. Look at Sergei. He is trying to sell a chess-playing platypus, for goodness sake."

"Damian." Nick's throat went dry. "Look at that side table." He pointed at the picture.

Damian looked. "We have a new connection, a new trail," he said.

For on the side table, among gold decanters and other items, stood the Chalice of Immortality.

CHAPTER

14

CLOUDS

B ACK AT THE HOTEL, NICK CHECKED ON HIS FATHER. HE still looked very, very sick. Nick wound up the music box and let it play, hoping that wherever his father was in the in-between world of the spell, he could hear it and be comforted.

As the music box softly played, Nick started thinking about the clouds he saw in Liberace's room. Why would a Magickeeper do such a thing? Ever since he'd arrived to live with his Russian family, all the Magickeepers had made it very clear that ordinary humans should never see their magic revealed. Suddenly, Nick experienced a flash of insight.

After he came to live at the Winter Palace, he tried to remember if he'd ever had visions or sensations of magic before. Sometimes, as a little kid, he used to get a feeling when something good was going to happen—like if he was going to hit a home run or nail a nollie on his skateboard. But that wasn't the same thing.

Sometimes, when he was a kid, he also would get a feeling in the pit of his stomach when something bad was going to happen. The first time he did an ollie on his skateboard, he had a very, *very* bad feeling he was going to fall flat on his face—and he was right. And just before he broke his arm while riding his board, he had a feeling he was going to smack the pavement. He also had a recurring bad feeling on report card days. But that wasn't the same thing as Gazing either.

Gazing meant he could see the past, the present, and the future. But most of the time, it was a jumble. He once told Isabella it was as if someone had made a movie. Then they had cut up the film, thrown the pieces up in the air like in a game of 52 Pickup, and spliced them all together again so the movie was a mess. The final film made no sense. It was out of order. That was what Gazing was like. Theo said he had to Gaze without expectation, with a pure heart and only good intentions, in order to see truly and accurately.

Sometimes, when Shadowkeepers were involved, Gazing gave Nick a horrible headache or made him feel sick to his stomach—so sick he couldn't breathe. But other times, he just felt dizzy or confused. This was one of those times.

Nick put his hands on the bed and concentrated. Then he felt himself flying. He was in the clouds.

They weren't painted clouds like those in Magickeeper murals. They were real clouds. He heard a loud noise— he was in a propeller plane, he decided, noisy, like one of Howard Hughes's old planes. Nick tried to steady himself, but the plane was…spinning? Clouds were swirling by him, faster and faster. He felt cold, and his teeth started chattering.

He swooped through the clouds. "Whoa!" he called out. "What's going on?" His stomach did flip-flops like he was on a roller coaster.

Spinning, spinning, spinning. Something was wrong. The plane was nose-diving. Spinning, spinning. Nick fell to his knees. He wanted this vision to stop, but he needed it to go on, because he was certain it had to do with the chalice.

And then—he saw a scarf fluttering. A white scarf, fluttering in the wind.

Nick blinked his eyes, and as fast as the vision had come to him, it stopped. He was back in his bedroom with his father. He was so dizzy that he had to wait a minute before trying to walk. Finally, his head stopped swirling.

"I'll be back, Dad," he whispered as he left the room and ran down the hall.

"Damian!" he called out. "Damian!" He looked in one room and then another before heading straight to Damian's study and bursting through the door.

His cousin looked up from a book he was reading. "What is it? Is it your father?"

Nick shook his head. "I had a vision. I know who has the chalice! Or at least, I *think* I do."

"Who?"

"Well, that's the thing. I don't know her name. But it was a woman I saw in Lady Daphne's shop. Both times I was in the shop, I felt someone staring at me. This woman—she was very…mysterious. She always wore a white scarf wrapped around her neck—kind of old-fashioned, I guess. And I always *felt* her staring at me. I can't explain it, but you know what I mean. I just knew. I saw a scarf—her scarf—in my vision. She knows something, Damian."

He paused for a breath, realizing he had said it all in one burst.

"Oh, and she was…she has something to do with *clouds*. Airplanes."

Damian narrowed his eyes. "A jet?"

"No. This was different. The planes in the clouds were like stunt planes. I heard propellers. I felt the air on my face. The scarf floated in the air, Damian."

His cousin pointed an index finger toward his bookshelves.

A book plucked itself from the shelf and floated through the air like a lazy leaf drifting in autumn. It landed on his desk and opened itself to a blank page. Damian uttered something, and ink began seeping out of the air onto the page like an oil spill before coming together in letters, and then a photograph.

"Is *this* the woman from the shop?"

Nick stared down. The woman had short, sandy-blond hair, freckles, a slight gap in her smile, and the same tanned, wind-burned skin of the woman from Lady Daphne's. Nick nodded, amazed. "I mean, she looks younger there, but that's her. Who is she?"

"This, Nick, is Amelia Earhart—her disappearance is only one of the greatest mysteries in history. We must go see Theo. He'll find her in one of his crystal balls. Come. We have no time to spare."

The Hawaiian Islands, March 18, 1937
Amelia Earhart stared dejectedly out the window of her hotel. The waters off the coast of Hawaii were a shade of blue that she had admired from the sky with a longing she could not quite describe.

She sighed. Her Lockheed Electra was going to need repairs and modifications, and for now, she would have to settle for a view of the beautiful waters from land. The waves swirled with white before crashing against coral rocks in a pounding surf over and over. Grass in a rich emerald shade covered the hotel lawn like a carpet. Palm trees swayed in the breeze. But here she was, behind a window, and she could only *see* the breeze, not feel it.

She walked away from the window and sat down on her bed. If she told the truth to herself, she felt like a prisoner in a glass house. A bird in a cage.

An adventurer at heart, the female aviator had become less a pilot in some ways and more an icon.

To pay for her flights and her planes, she endorsed suitcases. She had been involved with choosing their design— she wasn't going to endorse just anything! She also had a clothing line. Young ladies aspired to look like her, dress like her. She had the angular, lean looks of a tomboy, and she dressed simply and effectively, with clean lines. Now, Amelia Earhart was a "look." Wherever she went, people recognized her and wanted her autograph. She couldn't recall the last time she had been in public and not found herself approached by throngs of people.

Her husband, publisher G. P. Putnam, was brilliant. She gave him that. He was the one to line up these deals that enabled her to get her plane in the air. He was a master manager. And their marriage, admittedly a mixture of business and convenience, had turned into a fond and loving bond. He had ensured her celebrity status, which meant her flights into the history books were now well funded. She no longer had to worry about being unable to afford to fly. She had flown across the Atlantic Ocean, in fact, and across North America—and back again. She had accomplished things that women of her generation could now hope to do, instead of being confined to kitchens and households. Amelia liked to think that somewhere, on farms or in small towns, little girls who wanted to fly planes could believe now that they could—that the skies and the air and the freedom they afforded were possible.

But all of this came with a price. And increasingly, her celebrity status made Amelia feel like the price was her soul.

She felt as if she had no escape.

She flopped back on the bed and stared at the ceiling. She shut her eyes. There was nothing like being in the sky, like piloting a plane through clouds and sky. Nothing like it at all.

Flying was a gift. Over her years in the air, she had seen the sun rising on the ocean and flocks of birds taking flight from shore. She had seen the seas capped with white waves, and the mosaic of green and blue changing colors over reefs.

She had seen a whale breaching on the horizon. She had seen fields of corn and wheat stretching for miles across the middle of America, and she finally understood what the song meant by "amber waves of grain." She had watched America's heartlands undulate with the movement of crops in the wind. She had felt the absolute *freedom* of the skies. It was where she was happiest.

Amelia heard a knock on her hotel room door. She got up and opened it, greeting her navigator, Fred Noonan.

"Any news?" she asked.

He shook his head, grim-faced. "At least two more days, Amelia."

"Darn it all!" she snapped. She saw the circles beneath his eyes and immediately wished she had bit her tongue. "I'm sorry, Fred. I know it's not your fault. It's just so frustrating. I know you're just as upset as I am. Are you hungry, Fred? Shall we go downstairs for dinner?"

He nodded, and the two of them went down to the dining room. It was very late—the kitchen was almost closing—and at their request, they were shown to a table at the very back of the restaurant where they could eat in relative anonymity.

After their meals were brought, Amelia picked at her food, pushing it around with her fork. "I hate being grounded."

"Me, too."

Amelia suddenly looked him in the eyes. "Do you ever wish for simpler times, Fred? When flying was just flying?"

He nodded. "More than you can know, Amelia. More than you can know."

"I miss the days when I was anonymous."

They sat there, the two of them, and Amelia was certain Fred understood how *trapped* she felt. She watched as busboys went home. She and Fred paid their bill, and Fred said, "Since we clearly won't be taking off tomorrow, shall we have a nightcap?"

She nodded, and the two of them walked into the hotel bar. The bartender grinned at them. "I know who you are," he said. He reached out a hand across the bar. "My name is Goga." He shook hands with Amelia and Fred.

"Goga?" Amelia asked. "That's an unusual name."

"It is a good Russian name." He smiled. "But I tell *most* people my name is Greg. And I hide my accent."

"I rather like your accent," she said. She and Fred ordered drinks.

"I know what troubles you both."

Fred laughed. "Ah, you fancy yourself a mind reader! Well, the whole island knows we're grounded here for repairs on our plane."

"No." Goga looked all around. The bar was completely empty. "I mean your *real* troubles. The troubles in your heart." Goga tapped his chest.

"So you *are* a mind reader, then," Amelia teased.

"Yes." He said it plainly, and Amelia was startled. This man was serious.

"You," he nodded at Fred, "wish you could run away from your second marriage. Wish you could fly all the time. Wish you didn't need money so desperately. And you," he nodded toward Amelia, "you wish to escape the trickiest thing in the world—the one thing that is impossible to escape."

"What's that?"

"You wish to escape *yourself*. Not the real Amelia. Not the girlhood Amelia, who loved to read and play the banjo. You wish to escape the Amelia who is owned by the world. You wish to just fly."

Amelia looked at the Russian. He had magnetic blue eyes, and he was very, very solemn in his pronouncements. It was as if he had really looked into her heart and soul.

"I can help you," he said in a firm voice.

"How can you do that?" she whispered, fascinated—and a little frightened—by the conversation.

"What if I said I could make you disappear? Make you and your plane invisible so you could spend the rest of your life flying? And no one would know. You could go where you wanted with complete freedom. You, Amelia, could go and hunt for another whale breaching on the horizon." She jumped slightly, startled that Goga really *did* seem to know her thoughts.

Fred looked at the man suspiciously. "You must be nipping at the bottle, Goga."

"I never touch the stuff."

Suddenly, Goga disappeared. One minute, he was there with Amelia and Fred. The next, he was gone.

"Where did he go?" Fred asked.

Goga rematerialized on the other side of the darkened room. "Here I am."

Amelia turned her head in the direction of the voice and stared at Goga. "How…how…?"

But the words had barely escaped her lips when he reappeared back behind the bar.

"There must be a trap door," Fred said.

"Come, find it." Goga laughed, throwing his arms wide as if to show that there was nothing up his sleeves.

Fred did just that—or tried to, anyway. He climbed down from his barstool and walked to the place where Goga had popped up. He went so far as to get down on his hands and knees, feeling along the carpet for a hidden latch or edge to a trap door. Then he stood up and walked behind the bar. He stamped his feet along the floor, even jumping up and down, looking for the secret to Goga's disappearance.

"All right. Then you must have an identical twin."

Goga tilted his head back and laughed. "My dear mama would tell you that *one* of me was more than enough."

"You must tell us," Fred implored him. "How did you do that?"

Goga grinned. He snapped his fingers and disappeared. An instant later, he reappeared. "Magic."

Amelia's face drained of color. She couldn't trust her eyes. She was certain what she was seeing was real—but it couldn't be!

"Then tell me," she said, her voice trembling, "even if we...believed your outlandish claims, why would you help us? What's in it for you?" She had learned from her husband to question the motives of anyone with a deal too good to be true.

"I have certain nefarious enemies searching for me."

"Well," Fred drawled, "it would seem to me that since you can make yourself appear and disappear so easily, it would be quite simple to elude them."

"Ah, that would be true if my enemies were ordinary mortals like yourselves. But they are not. They are as powerful as I am—perhaps more so."

Amelia leaned an elbow on the bar, fascinated. This had all the makings of the most extraordinary adventure ever. "Go on."

"I have a certain object...I need it kept safe. And I need it off this island within a few days. If my sources are correct, my enemies will soon be arriving. In exchange for granting both of you the freedom to fly the skies invisibly—I shall entrust you with a chalice. You must ask no questions about it. You must not drink from it. And you must not reveal its existence to anyone. You will disappear with the chalice…and sometime in the future, I will come and retrieve it. Perhaps at that time, you will wish to come back from your adventure. And what a story that will make!"

Amelia looked at Fred. All her life, she had longed for adventure—even a touch of danger. And this strange, magical man had just offered her the chance of a *hundred* lifetimes.

"Fred?" She cocked an eyebrow at her navigator, who grinned.

"I'm game," he said.

Amelia reached her hand across the bar. "You have a deal, Goga."

The two of them shook on it, and Amelia Earhart, "Lady Lindy" of the skies, became deliriously excited at the thought of the freedom she would now be able to enjoy. It was as if her very breath was lighter now.

THE LADY IN THE WHITE SCARF

*T*HEO SAID, "WE MUST GO BACK TO ENGLAND AT ONCE! Kolya, you're to come with Damian and me. We're nearing the end of the chalice's twisted path."

Damian found Irina, Isabella's older sister, and told her to make sure all of the family returned to the casino. The chalice's path had become clearer and led back to the sausage shop, of all places.

Damian and Theo cast spells, and instantly, Nick and his two older cousins were back in Lady Daphne's bed and breakfast, emerging out of the hall closet in the entryway. They went downstairs and found Lady Daphne in her kitchen having a cup of hot tea and a scone, a wolf curled at her feet.

"Blimey, duckies! You're back! Just dropping in my closets, are you now? I was having a cup of tea before bedtime," she chuckled. "The many surprises of this inn!"

Nick was grateful that she was in a flannel nightgown and curlers—and not her meat-covered apron. He leaned down and hugged her, happy to avoid the sausage bits.

"Lady Daphne," he said anxiously, "we need to see a woman who is a customer at your tea shop. She always sits at the same table, and she wears a white scarf. Do you know who I'm talking about?"

"I know precisely whom you wish to see. Her name is Millie."

Nick looked at Theo and Damian. "That must be her nickname."

"Where can we find her?" Theo asked. "It is very, very important."

"Why, right upstairs. She stays in Room C."

Nick hugged Lady Daphne again. "Thanks!"

The three of them bounded up the stairs. Nick knocked on the wooden door of Room C. There was silence for a few moments, and then the door opened wide. Standing there was the woman from the crystal ball.

"I've been expecting you," she said softly. "Come in."

Nick looked at each of his cousins and stepped into her room. They followed.

Amelia Earhart—a little older than her pictures, but with the same slightly shy smile—gestured toward chairs around a small table. The four of them sat down.

"Expecting us?" Nick asked.

"I knew someday the right guardian would come. I know of your bravery. I know about the wolves. I thought you would be the one."

"You've been missing...all this time?" Nick asked, still amazed that she was Amelia Earhart.

"Yes. Fred and I—our plane disappeared over the Pacific. After a search, my husband had me declared legally dead. He remarried a few months later, thus assuaging any guilt I felt over my bit of deception." She smiled wryly at them.

"Amelia—" Nick started to speak.

"Call me Millie," she said. "It's the name I had as a little girl—my sister gave me that nickname."

Nick said, "How? How have you been able to hide all this time? And...do you have the chalice?"

Theo said, "Did you know we were here for it? We need it, Millie. Nick's father...he's under a very, very deadly spell. Do you know the power of the chalice?"

She nodded. "I can take you to the chalice. But first, a story. And then a promise from you, before I lead you to it."

Nick nodded. "Whatever promise you need. Please..." He thought of his father's translucent skin. "I don't know how much time we have."

"Fred Noonan and I made a deal—a deal with man named Goga. We took the chalice and took to the skies, and he arranged for us to simply disappear. At the time," she smiled ruefully, "I felt trapped by my life. I know it sounds crazy, but I was a younger woman then. I was impetuous. I wanted to fly. I didn't ask to become an icon." She played with her white scarf. "I just like wearing this. I didn't expect that suddenly scarves like this would be all the rage with girls who looked up to me."

She sighed and put her hands in her lap. "I made the choice of an impetuous woman without thinking through all the details. All my life I'd been so headstrong. No one could tell me anything differently. So I made the decision rashly. At first, the freedom was delightful. Fred and I simply disappeared, along with the plane, over the middle of the ocean. He and I…" She laughed. "We flew around the world. We saw things that still sustain me. We were delirious with the sheer joy of flying again."

"And the chalice?" Theo asked.

"The chalice rode with us in the cockpit. I kept it in a velvet pouch—the same one it was in when Goga gave it to us. We expected that one day, that strange Russian would simply appear and ask for it back. Some nights, Fred and I would sit on whatever airfield we had landed at, and we would marvel at the strange turn our lives had taken. The magic was wonderful. I mean, we would sometimes just walk into a restaurant and steal plates of delicious food. We'd fuel our plane without being seen. We lived like vagabonds, and

I have no doubt that the people at the airfields we went to, the places we visited, thought a pair of mischievous ghosts had done what we had just done. And some nights, we pondered just what that chalice was—we knew it had to have something to do with magic."

"You were curious, of course," Damian said.

"Indeed. And then—then Fred and I began to see strange things on our adventures. We saw what I now know are Shadowkeepers. We would sense them, these shadowy creatures, and we were always just a few steps ahead of them, it seemed."

"What did they look like?" Theo asked.

"Sometimes, I thought they looked like winged demons. Other times, it just seemed as if darkness was encroaching on us. When I saw them, a chill passed over me that I could not warm up from. We'd be taking off for the air as they arrived at an airfield. Occasionally, I saw one fly across the moon like a shadow—the wing span was perhaps thirteen feet. We knew we could not keep ahead of them forever. And then Fred and I realized there was a flaw in Goga's plan."

"What was that?" Damian asked.

"We had no way to contact him. We were waiting for him to come to us—but we didn't know when that might be. So we flew back to Hawaii to try to track him down, and there, we learned he had been killed."

"How?" Nick asked.

"In the attack on Pearl Harbor. It wasn't even a Shadowkeeper that got him. In the strangest of turns in our already strange adventure, he was killed by the evil of regular people, not the evil of the Shadowkeepers. So now Fred and I were stuck. Of course, thinking about it now, remembering it, I can't believe we were so foolish." She put her hands on the table and shook her head.

Theo reached out and patted her hand. "Magic can do that. It's bewildering. It's exciting. It's intoxicating. It's seductive. Do not feel ashamed, Millie. Magic has been the undoing of many a mortal, and many a Magickeeper."

"Fred took it hardest, but we decided to make the best of it. However, one day, we were attacked by Shadowkeepers. They came at us while we slept in sleeping bags beside our plane, here in England."

"Was there a man among them?" Theo asked.

"No. These were tall, almost seven feet, I think, with a wide wingspan. They flew, like the ones I had seen fly across the moon, on leathery wings. Their faces were *almost* human, though distorted. And their oily skin seemed to drip this foul-smelling—" She wrinkled her nose. "I suppose you know what they smell like."

Nick nodded. "Sure do. Like egg salad left on a school bus in June!"

Millie laughed. "Yes, I believe so."

"So what happened?" Theo asked gently.

"Fred was killed, and the chalice was stolen. I escaped by reaching my plane and locking myself in the cockpit. But once they had the chalice, they didn't seem to care much about me." She looked up, eyes teary. "Over time, since we only had each other, Fred had become my best friend. Losing him—it was devastating."

She was silent for several long minutes. "But I didn't become a pilot—didn't take the risks I took, didn't change aviation history for women—for nothing. I am Amelia Earhart, after all. So I made it my life's mission to find out about the chalice, to find out more about the magic world. That's what I have been doing all these years. I have been to Las Vegas. I have been in a room with Howard Hughes. I followed the trail wherever it led me."

"But...we see you now. How did you become un-invisible again?" Nick asked.

"I followed the trail to Las Vegas, where I saw Howard Hughes. And then I heard a rumor about a Magical Curiosity Shoppe."

"Madame B.!"

"Yes. She helped me attain my human form again. Gave me several potions. It was she who told me about the power of the chalice, what it could do. Since I had resisted its powers, she felt that I would be an acceptable guardian for it. I was always just a few steps behind the chalice. And then I heard of a Magickeeper—a painter named Vadim."

"I know him," Damian practically growled. "He painted the ceiling in my casino."

"And he painted a ceiling for Liberace. He stole the chalice from Liberace, who, as near as I can figure it, acquired it from one of Howard Hughes's inner circle, some of whom were stealing from him. Vadim took the chalice, but he also stole one of Liberace's silver candelabra and a painting! He was a thief, and I had the feeling that perhaps he did not know what he was in possession of. I used one of Madame B.'s potions to temporarily cause him to fall into a deep sleep."

Theo smiled. "Clever. The Sleeping Beauty potion."

She nodded. "And then I stole the chalice back."

"It's a shame I was not there," snarled Damian. "The perpetrator would have suffered. Vadim would have been turned into a piglet, and he would already be *bacon* by now!"

Millie stared up at them, eyes glistening. "I wanted to wait until I found someone I could trust, truly trust to become its new caretaker."

"So you'll take us to it?" Nick asked.

"I will."

SHAKESPEARE'S BONES

*T*HAT NIGHT, UNDER A STILL AND STARLESS SKY, NICK, Theo, Damian, and Millie walked down a silent path lined with lime trees leading to Holy Trinity Church in Stratford-upon-Avon. They entered the doors and passed through archways, their footsteps echoing on the marble.

Nick looked at the stained glass windows and the carvings in marble. The cavernous ceilings of the nave carried every sound high and hushed. Damian materialized a torch to lead the way.

They walked through the whole church until they stood at the sanctuary behind a brass railing.

"Here lies William Shakespeare," Millie said. "He bought the rights to care for the chancel, and therefore, he had the right to be buried in this very building."

Nick stared down. There was a flat stone, not like any grave he had ever seen. "So he's in there?"

"Actually," Theo said. "It's Shakespeare; his wife, Anne Hathaway; and their daughter, Suzanna. His son-in-law too. All together for eternity."

"What does it say on his grave?" Nick asked. There were letters carved into the old stone, but in the dim torchlight, he could just barely make them out.

Millie lifted her head, reciting the words, apparently from memory, in a clear voice.

> *Good frend for Jesus sake forebeare,*
> *To digg the dust encloased heare.*
> *Blese be y man y spares thes stones,*
> *And curst…*

"So there's a curse on the grave?" Nick interrupted.

"Yes," Millie said. "And as I researched the Chalice of Immortality and saw its danger and its power, I followed it all the way back to William Shakespeare. Once I had it in my possession again, I thought I would bring it full circle to rest with the great playwright. He placed this curse on his grave so that grave robbers would not disturb his bones at a time when grave robbing was a common crime."

"We know," Nick said. "Sir Arthur Conan Doyle got

it from the heir of a doctor who bought bones from grave robbers."

"Worse," Millie said, "in Shakespeare's time, sometimes people bought the right to a grave and just put the new bones of the dead over the older ones. Shakespeare feared, given his fame, that his bones might be stolen and sold. Or that some stranger would be buried on top of him." She shuddered.

"So he's really in there?" Nick asked.

"He's really in there. The curse worked. Until me, of course, but I wasn't *robbing* Shakespeare's bones, I was merely putting something there to rest with him—something I needed kept safe." She reached out and took Nick's hand. "Look at my face, Nick."

He stared at the weathered face of Amelia Earhart. In her eyes, he still saw the tomboy she had been once, young and longing for the skies.

"Once mortals mingle with Magickeepers, they age differently, slower. I am very old, though I don't look it—not entirely. But even I know that immortality is wrong, Nick. It is not the natural order of things. We are all meant to die one day, even great men like Shakespeare. Even"—her voice choked off a little—"great friends like Fred Noonan. I miss him still, but I understand that people live, and people die. And I need to be sure that you understand that, too."

"I do. I really do. I don't want my father to die from a

spell. I wish my mother hadn't died at Rasputin's hand. Somehow, I think my life would have been very different if she hadn't died. But I understand that someday, we all die. I just want it to be when it's *supposed* to happen, not because a Shadowkeeper has worked evil magic."

"You must make me one promise."

"What?"

"Heal your father, then lock this chalice away so no more lives are lost because of it."

Nick looked at Theo, who nodded.

"Of course, Millie," Nick replied. The Winter Palace Hotel and Casino had a near-impenetrable vault where relics were kept.

"And don't drink of it yourself," she added.

"I won't."

"I mean it. I sipped water from it, one time. Still not aware of its full power. And I could feel it taking hold of me. That night, every time I shut my eyes, I saw the chalice in my mind, its gold shimmering, its ruby calling me like a siren's song. I heard it whispering, *Drink*. I decided then the chalice was far better resting with someone *already* dead, like Shakespeare, than someone living who might be tempted by it."

She exhaled. "All right, then, my long adventure comes to an end tonight. I can live out the rest of my days at Lady

Daphne's. Go ahead, Theo…open the grave. I had to do it with a crowbar. I trust you can do it far more easily."

Theo waved his arms, uttering a spell in rapid-fire Russian. The top slab lifted with a grating sound of stone rubbing against stone.

"Go on, Nick," Theo commanded. "Get the chalice."

Nick peered in at the tomb of Shakespeare. Dusty bones, teeth, a skull, and a velvet pouch. "Sorry, sir," he whispered. He knelt next to the now-open grave and reached his hand into its darkness. He found the hand and finger bones clutching the velvet bag that Millie had placed in the grave. With a shudder, he gently dislodged the bag and pulled it out.

Theo replaced the slab, which closed with a resounding thud. He uttered another spell, then translated. "I said, 'May your bones not be disturbed for another thousand years.'"

Nick opened the black velvet bag. The large chalice gleamed, giving off its own pulsing light and energy. The gold was the shiniest he had ever seen.

"We have it at last," he whispered. As he held the chalice, he flashed on a vision of its one-time guardian, William Shakespeare.

Stratford-upon-Avon, March 25, 1616
William Shakespeare sat at his desk, composing his last will and testament with a long quill pen. His handwriting was slightly unsure, as it was a terrible premonition he had that was causing him to draft his will. As he wrote, he sipped from the chalice on his desk. He stroked the chalice, his most wondrous chalice. His most hated chalice.

Like a battle with a dangerous foe, the chalice represented turmoil for Shakespeare. He was convinced that the chalice was the *only* thing that kept the words flowing through him. When he drank from the chalice, new ideas flooded his mind. His sonnets seemed to compose themselves. They would rush into him—precious words.

In fact, the chalice, he was now certain, was the reason he was a playwright—the reason he had fame. As the world's greatest playwright and part-owner of his own theater company, he felt a little bit like a fraud. And this displeased him.

How had this happened? At one time, he was *certain* the words were his own. But now? Now he was not so certain. He cursed the day the chalice came into his life.

And yet, he could not part with it. *Never!* The idea, the very idea, filled him with a cold dread.

Hamlet. Act five, scene two. He had written of a poison in the chalice meant for Hamlet—who refused to drink from it. Shakespeare had found ways to honor the chalice in his plays.

Sometimes, it was only in a party scene. But sometimes, the chalice played a real and integral part. Shakespeare would sit with the crowd in disguise as he had that first time with *Romeo and Juliet* and smile bemusedly because the audience had no idea.

He heard a knock on his door and assumed it was his servant.

"You may enter," he called out.

But instead of his servant, in stepped the Russian, Fyodor.

Shakespeare gasped. "How long it has been, my friend, how long? I scarce believe it is you. Are you a ghost, come to frighten me to death?" Shakespeare looked down at his will and then up at Fyodor. It had been many years since he'd seen the Russian, but the man had not aged a day. How was that possible?

"I have come for the chalice, William."

Shakespeare reflexively grabbed the chalice and clutched it to his breast.

"No! You must not. No! You shall not!"

"You were intended as its guardian for a brief time, but admittedly, my enemies made my return here one of great difficulty."

"No." Shakespeare felt an icy chill settle over his heart. This could not be happening. He would never be able to write another word—not without his beloved chalice. His accursed chalice! There was a true battle inside him, but he could not give the cup to the Russian.

"I can see that it has a power over you," Fyodor said.

"It is my life! The chalice makes my words possible. It fills me with inspiration. *Hamlet, Henry VIII, Othello*...my greatest plays were created while I imbibed from the chalice. This chalice has brought me acclaim."

"No," the Russian said darkly. "You composed those words! You did! You are in the chalice's possession. I should not have left it here this long. This will be painful, but I must take it from you."

"No! I shall murder you with my own hand rather than let you take this chalice!"

"Do you hear yourself, William Shakespeare? Look at your trembling hand, your sweating brow! Look! Look at what you have become—a slave."

"I am no slave."

"You are. A slave to this chalice. You must let it go, William. You must. Now hand it to me."

Still Shakespeare clutched it to his bosom.

"I said, hand it to me!" Fyodor spoke Russian words, some sort of spell, Shakespeare surmised. Inside his very room, it thundered. Lightning flashed. The room went dark. And when the thunder and lightning had stopped and his lantern was again lit, Shakespeare realized that Fyodor had the chalice. He had wrested it from him.

"Please, please, I beg of you! Do not take it!"

"No," Fyodor said, shaking his head sadly. "It is too dangerous."

With that, the Russian walked out of the room to the anguished cries of William Shakespeare.

Alone, without his chalice, Shakespeare thought he might weep. A single tear splashed down on his will. He picked up his quill pen and continued, deciding which of his heirs would inherit his things.

When he was done, he stared down at his last will and testament.

Shakespeare whispered, "I might as well die. Without my chalice, I am nothing."

He placed his quill pen on the desk and stared forlornly out the window. He was fifty-two years old.

And in exactly four weeks, though he was not ill, William Shakespeare died.

Of a broken heart.

✧　✧　✧

Nick blinked, out of breath. He relayed the vision he had, then said, "Such a sad end." He stood up and looked at Millie. "I don't know how to thank you."

"Thank me by being a good guardian of the chalice, Nick. Don't let it destroy you. Don't allow it to muddle your head or to bond with you. It's too dangerous."

Nick nodded. "I won't." Then he looked at Theo. "I hope the chalice is as powerful—for just this one time—as I need it to be."

Theo reached out to touch the chalice. "It is." He shut his eyes and inhaled, using magical senses. He spoke, almost in a whisper. "Its origins are in Egypt at the time of Ramses II. He was, like all the pharaohs, powerful and omnipotent, and often ruthless. When he discovered a plot to assassinate him, he condemned all the conspirators—including one of his wives—to death. One of those condemned to die was a magician. The method of execution was to force the condemned to commit suicide."

Nick shuddered , remembering Theo's lesson on Socrates, the philosopher who was sentenced to drink poison.

"On the eve of the execution, three Magickeepers assembled under cover of darkness. Speaking the most powerful incantations over the chalice, uniting the magic of all three and their bloodline, they created a chalice that would render the magician into death to be revived later when they exhumed him from his tomb. But because their spell interfered with life and death, they realized, once they saved their friend, that the chalice would need to be guarded. It had powers of immortality, powers over death that no Magickeeper—or ordinary mortal—should have. Magicians are not meant to be gods."

Millie whispered, "Now you know why I had to be so careful about who took possession of the chalice."

Nick hugged Millie. "I promise I will be a good guardian."
"I can tell."

"We have to go now, Millie." He clutched the chalice and the four of them ran from the church.

"Theo, look!"

The wolves were waiting for them. Seven of them sat like obedient dogs in the middle of the stone pathway between the lime trees. They howled. But without Isabella, Nick had no idea what the wolves were saying to them.

"If they are here, they must want to warn us about something," Nick said. There was no other logical explanation. "Let's get Millie back to Lady Daphne's, and then we must fly home."

They raced through the empty streets, wolves following them, paws scraping on the stone pathways, to Lady Daphne's, and Nick saw, standing on the bed and breakfast's thatched roof, a figure dressed in a black monk's habit. He hovered like a ghost and stared down at them.

Rasputin!

"Millie," Damian commanded, "you need to come with us. We'll return you when it's safe. But for now, we need to get the chalice to America, and you should remain with us."

She nodded, but at that moment, Rasputin uttered a spell, and the wolves' beastly nature took over. One lunged at Millie and bit her hand. She shrieked in pain, and in the commotion, the blood, and the snarling of wolves, Nick saw Damian rise up and fly toward Rasputin. But then behind Rasputin, dozens of winged Shadowkeepers swooped down in an all-out attack. Nick watched as his two cousins fought with a flurry of side kicks and flames.

Nick created a fire circle around him and Millie so he could help tend to her injury while keeping the wolves at bay. Then he felt a cold chill like he had never felt before.

He looked up just as Rasputin flew straight at him and pressed his hand over Nick's mouth.

And then the world went utterly dark.

MIND BENDING

ICK'S HEAD POUNDED. HE OPENED HIS EYES, BUT HE HAD no idea where he was. The room spun in dizzying circles that reminded him of the visions he had of Amelia Earhart's spiraling plane. But this was far worse, because he was suffocating. So he reminded himself to *breathe*.

That's better, he thought to himself. He blinked several times. Then he left his eyes open and tried to figure out just where the heck he was. But he quickly realized he was not anywhere he had ever been before.

He wondered, for real, if he was on another planet.

Around him, long stalagmites and stalactites grew in complex formations. He heard dripping sounds, like water constantly trickling. And he was cold—very, very cold. He shivered. The air smelled funny.

The landscape of this strange planet or whatever was barren. No trees grew. No grass. He was aware of snowflake-like growths on the wall. He tried to touch one, but his arms ached so much that he could not move them.

"What the heck?" he mouthed aloud. He turned his head gingerly and saw a lake—a lake of black water. *All right,* he thought. There was water on this planet.

But—no sky? Nick stared straight above him. There were more snowflake-like growths, but no sky. No moon. No stars. Certainly, no sun. Torches burned in holders on the wall.

He started remembering the simple acronym he'd learned in third grade to recall the planets. *My Very Evil Mother Just Showed Us Nine Planets. Mercury, Venus, Earth, Mars, Jupiter, Saturn, Uranus, Neptune, Pluto.* He wondered, *Does it matter that Pluto isn't considered a planet anymore?*

Nick struggled to focus his eyes and remember all the planets. He thought he might throw up. Which planet was he on?

From a long way off, he heard the sound of paws padding on rock. Nick rolled over and tried to sit up. He was resting on a damp rock—he seemed to be bound there by some spell. His head spun, and he leaned over and retched.

Then he heard Rasputin's voice.

"Ahh, I see our guest has awakened."

The crazed monk stood, framed by the light of a torch.

Next to him was a wolf, but behind him, Nick saw the leathery shapes of Shadowkeepers.

"Where are my cousins? Where is Millie?"

"If they even survived, which I seriously doubt, you are someplace Damian and Theo will never find you, I'm afraid. The Kungur Ice Caves."

"What?" Nick croaked dryly. "What ice caves?"

"Caves in Mother Russia. Far *beneath* Mother Russia, I should say. No one will hear you *scream*. No one but I shall know how deeply you will suffer. No one will see you as I force you to consider just whose side you want to be on. You are mine, little Nicholai Rostov."

"I'm not little," Nick said. "You're really starting to get on my nerves." He gritted his teeth, bile still burning the back of his throat. "Give me back the chalice."

The monk laughed. "Or what? Your false bravado won't do anything, Nick."

Nick swallowed and tried to think of how he could escape.

"You fell right into my trap. What would compel the boy, the prince of the Magickeepers, to find me the chalice I desired, the chalice that would seal my immortality forever? What would compel him to find this relic for me? Who would he be willing to move heaven and earth to save? There were a few choices. Should I cast the spell between life and death on dear, sweet little Isabella?" He said the words mockingly. "She who protects the animals? The one who so selfishly released my wolves?"

At the word *wolves*, the beast next to Rasputin snarled. Nick stared at the crazed monk. The Grand Duchess had told him stories about Rasputin, about how his eyes were marred by insanity and evil. She was right. Only, if it were possible, he was more murderous now.

"Isabella is a spunky one. And she is your best friend. But there is that *tiger* of hers to contend with. I don't like tigers. So I thought…should I cast the spell on Theo? Ah, Theo, my despised nemesis. He should have rightfully led the family, but I discovered merely killing the woman he cared about was enough to make him retreat to that classroom of his, to his books and spells. Theo isn't the Magickeeper he once was. He is too much the scholar, too much the historian. The teacher. And I know you love him, but no, no, no, he was not the right choice."

Nick didn't want to listen to anymore.

"Or perhaps the Grand Duchess? But…such a weakling now. Not worthy of my attentions. She's positively ancient. My biggest regret is I didn't kill her along with her family when they were murdered in cold blood." Rasputin paced slightly. "Or maybe Damian. Should I cast this spell on him? A family clan without a leader would render them confused, would it not? In disarray. I rather liked the thought." Rasputin's voice was gravelly.

"You will pay for this!" Nick said.

The monk, his black clothes moth-eaten and musty, threw his head back and laughed. "But then I decided, no. I thought about a boy who grew up without a mother. No one to teach him his ABCs and 1-2-3s—evident from your report card, no less. What would that boy be like? And even if he thought his father was a failed magician, he would have all his childhood memories with that man. So I decided that when I destroyed Madame B.'s shop, the spell would be cast—and you would have to find the chalice. You would find it because you are a clever boy, perhaps the cleverest of all. And indeed, you have brought me precisely what I need to rule forever."

He held up the chalice, admiring its shining beauty. "I suppose I should thank you. But instead, I'm going to make you suffer."

Nick suddenly felt a stabbing pain in his temples. He had never felt pain like that before. Clutching his head, he fell to the floor. The wolf strained at its leash. Nick lifted his arms up to shield his face from the wolf's teeth. The world started swimming in front of him. The pain in his head intensified.

"Hurt enough for you?" Rasputin asked. "Why don't you beg me to make it stop?"

"Never!"

Rasputin neared. The Shadowkeepers stayed in the dark

recesses of the cavern. Rasputin raised a finger. The pounding in Nick's head subsided, and he caught his breath.

"Why do you use your power for evil and not good?" Nick asked. "Why did you hurt the Grand Duchess's family? Why? You don't have to be this way. Why did you leave the family tree?" He hated to think he was actually *related* to the monk, way back in the far recesses of his family history. The first night Damian kidnapped him, he had shown him the family tree, and in the area where Rasputin was, the branches were charred and blackened.

"But I *do* have to be this way," Rasputin sneered. "It is my nature. And you may not believe it, but it is your nature, too! You're just too blinded by love for your newfound family to see it. You need to think back to the loneliness, to the way the other children in school treated you when your clothes were just a little too shabby."

Despite everything Nick knew about the monk, he felt his head hurting, and his mind…involuntarily opened to the monk.

Rasputin reached out a hand to Nick's head and placed his fingers at Nick's temple. Nick couldn't fight him. It was as if the monk's fingers were made of the strongest stone.

"Now, my dear Kolya, I want to discover what makes you love. I find it curious. You could have all the power in the magic world. You could bring kings and presidents to their knees. You could rule the planet, have riches beyond your wildest dreams. But instead, you stay inside a hotel and cater to crowds of *tourists*." He spat the word. "Why? Only the foolishness of love makes you do that. And now I shall see for myself why that is."

Nick gasped. He saw stars, honest-to-goodness stars, as Rasputin pressed his fingers into his temples. And then, just like in Gazing, his world spun in a kaleidoscope of out-of-order images.

☆　☆　☆

"Look at him, darling," his mother cooed. "He's having his first taste of cereal. Snap a picture so we remember this day."

His father stood with a camera, a lopsided, adoring grin on his face. "Smile, my precious little boy. Say cheese."

Snap.

Flash.

The camera took his picture. His mother leaned over and kissed the top of his head. She smelled like jasmine perfume. "I've never been so happy in my entire life." She looked at his father. "I love you so much."

"I love you, too."

"I wish we could stay here forever. Just freeze this moment—always safe, always happy. Just this perfect moment for the three of us."

His father reached out and squeezed her hand. "We're safe, darling. I won't let anything happen to you or our son." His father leaned down and kissed his head. "Don't babies smell like heaven?"

His father rocked him. "She's gone, baby Kolya. She's dead, and now I think my heart is broken." He let out a small sob. "But I promise you, I will never, ever, ever leave you."

The TV cast his father in a bluish light. It droned on and on, keeping them company in the night. Rather than put him to bed in his crib, his father just held him all night long until he fell asleep, his head to one side, still clutching Nick tightly in his arms.

"He's walking!" Grandpa beamed. "A chip off the old block. He takes after me."

"Because he's walking, Gustav?" his father said, laughing. "Walking? I mean, I walk, too, you know."

"Ahh, but it's how he walks. With panache. With style!"

"I give up." His father threw up his hands teasingly. They watched him toddle toward a table and bang with blocks, making a racket. But neither man shushed him.

"He's a gift. From her, from Tatyana." His grandfather scooped Nick up in his burly arms. "People die, but if they have children, they go on. They live forever, in some way."

✿ ✿ ✿

"I don't get it," Nick whined. "Math is too hard for me."

"Nothing is too hard for you, Kolya," his father soothed. "You're brilliant."

"I'm not! Math is too hard for me. Look at these multiplication tables. It's the twelves! It's like—a foreign language."

"Ah, but I never told you about your mother, did I? She could speak six languages." He held up his hand as he counted off on his fingers. "English, Russian, Polish, Greek, Latin...and Multiplication Tables."

Nick looked up from his tear-stained homework. "Come on, Dad. I'm not like her. She must have been really smart. I'm not smart."

"You are, though." He said it so earnestly. "And did I tell you that you're special?"

Nick shrugged, shoulders hunched.

"Show me your palm."

Nick held out his hand.

His father pointed. "Now, I'm no palm reader. That's for your mother's family. They're a little...eccentric. But I do know *this. You have a special star in your palm somewhere...and it means—well, it means you are special and brilliant. Your mother told me that. And I know all parents say their kids are special and brave and brilliant, but you really are. So you can do this."*

Nick nodded. "Sure."

"Try again. For me."

"All right. Twelve times nine is...is...108."

His father beamed. "See?" He high-fived him. "I told you!"

✩ ✩ ✩

"I had a bad dream!" Nick sat up, sweating. "I saw a man with... crazy eyes, and he was coming in my room."

His father sat down on his bed. "That's the third nightmare this month. Maybe I should stop doing my act. Get a nine-to-five job, so I'm always here at night. It seems like these nightmares come more and more frequently."

"But you have to work nights. You're a magician."

"Ahh, your mother completed the act. Since then, I've lost my love for it. And honestly, Kolya, I would rather work days—even at a job I hate—than think of you having these horrific nightmares with no one here to sit with you. In the end, you are more important than anything in my life. I'll sell insurance. I'll butcher meat! I'll sell shoes or...be a waiter. I don't care. I just want you to feel safe."

"Don't do that. You're a magician. It's what you do."

"Then maybe I can ask your grandfather to stay here most nights. He can sleep on the pull-out couch."

Nick grinned at his dad. *"I think I'll give him my bed. He'd break the pull-out. Plus he snores!"*

His father laughed. *"Ol' Gustav is a piece of work, but he loves you, and I know he would stay here with you, at least until you're over these nightmares."* His father mussed his hair affectionately. *"We both love you, you know."*

"Grandpa... if I eat another bite, I just might fall over."

"Ahh! Carrying on the family tradition of the all-you-can-eat buffet. I love you, kid."

"I love you, too."

"Now listen to me...for your thirteenth birthday, we're going to have quite an adventure."

"Really? Did you get tickets to the magic show at the Winter Palace Hotel and Casino?"

"Now that would be something, considering they're sold out years in advance. No...not that. But something very, very fun!"

✿ ✿ ✿

"*I must be dreaming,*" *Nick whispered, his heart pounding so hard, he wondered if that had been the thumping sound he heard.*

"*'Fraid not, Nicholai. Time to fly,*" *Damian said, waving his hand. When Nick woke up, he was in Damian's library. Clouds floated overhead.*

✫ ✫ ✫

"*It's a spark. Irina told me that when a Magickeeper is born, a shining star glows deep down inside the child. Part of its flicker is the gift the child inherits, and part is a Magickeeper birthright. Have you not noticed that Magickeepers seem to age differently than humans?*"

Nick nodded. "Yeah. Damian and Theo, they look much younger than they are. And the Grand Duchess—she's really old, but she's still alive."

"*It's the magic part of us. I have it. You have it. But child essence is very powerful, Nick. It's innocent. It's the closest people are in their lifetime to the purity of who they are supposed to be.*"

✫ ✫ ✫

Ochi chornyye, ochi strastnyye,
Ochi zhguchiye i prekrasnyye.
Kak lyublyu ya vas, kak boyus' ya vas,
Znat' uvidel vas ya v nedobryi chas.

✩ ✩ ✩

Rasputin sneered again. "Love! It's a completely impractical emotion. It will be your downfall, Kolya—because you will either join me or die tonight! I have seen inside your heart. I know how to destroy you!"

JUST A SIP

NICK STARED UP AT THE MADMAN, BUT HE KNEW HE WOULD never betray his family.

"Do you want to know how Tatyana died?" Rasputin asked.

Nick shook his head. Did it matter?

"She suffered."

"I hate you!" Nick spat. As soon as he said that, the Shadowkeepers hissed and came closer.

"They thrive on hatred. Good," Rasputin soothed. "Good. *Feed* their souls."

"They have no souls," Nick said. His head ached. He felt like even his *eyelashes* hurt.

"Let me give you just a taste of her suffering."

The monk laid his hands on Nick's chest. Nick felt a stabbing pain like lightning flash in his chest then fan out to his extremities. He hurt. He hurt like he had never hurt in his life—not even the time he had gotten the flu, and it had turned into pneumonia and he had ended up in the hospital.

"I will offer you, one last time, the opportunity to rule beside me. Imagine vast riches. Power. Control. Imagine kings bowing before you. Imagine moving through time and space, unfettered by the rules of ordinary mortals."

"No…thank…you…" Nick hissed through his teeth.

"I can't let you fulfill the prophecy."

With the rock digging into his spine and sending chills up into his skull, Nick asked, "What prophecy? Maybe I am not even part of the prophecy!"

"Fool."

Rasputin tilted his head back, and his next words he uttered were so hate-filled, Nick saw his body shudder with each syllable.

A child of lineage and love
Shall forever doom the monk of hate.
A mother's sacrifice and love
Shall forever destroy the legacy of hate.
And fires of magic and love
Shall consume shadows for eternity
And lead in light forever.

"And you think I am the 'child of love'? That's a stretch."

"Don't try to deflect what I know to be true. I should have killed you in your crib, you vile brat."

"Theo and Damian will find me. You won't get away with this."

"Do you think they survived that fight? Just the two of them against so many of my minions? And they will come just like when they rescued your mother? Instead, they led me to her—just as you have brought me the chalice so that I may live forever."

"The chalice is dangerous. Don't you know what it did to Howard Hughes? How it tried to control Sir Arthur Conan Doyle? How it made William Shakespeare doubt his own gift with words? It will..." Nick fumbled for words. It would what? Make him crazy? He was already insane.

"Yes or no, Nicholai Rostov? Join me or die!"

"Never!" Nick spat the word.

At that, Rasputin touched him, and a black oil began coating his feet. Nick kicked his legs, but as the oil traveled up his body, he found it was paralyzing him.

"Imagine her terror! You can imagine it, can't you? Her dying thoughts were of you. I saw into her mind! Just as your dying thoughts will be of that family you love so much. *Feel it consuming you. Suffer.*"

As the oil coated him, Nick's muscles tensed and then felt like they were on fire. Finally, he could bear it no longer, and he let out a scream, which in turn made the Shadowkeepers howl. Their sounds echoed off the cavern walls.

Rasputin neared and stood over him. "Hurts, doesn't it?"

The oil now covered Nick's stomach. The Shadowkeepers neared, their teeth gleaming in the torchlight.

The oil now spread over Nick's chest, and he couldn't breathe. He wanted to breathe, but his ribs were paralyzed.

Finally, the oil coated his neck, as if a boa constrictor had wrapped itself around his throat.

Only Nick's head remained, and he knew the oil would soon slide into his mouth. The oil crept up his chin.

And then it stopped.

Rasputin held up the chalice.

"One sip and you will be restored. Are you prepared to join me, Nick?"

Nick thought of the chalice's hold on people. He thought of what he had seen at Shakespeare's grave. And he thought of the promise he had made to Millie.

"No. I will not."

"You are prepared to die rather than join me?"

"I am."

The monk brought the chalice to Nick's lips. But the young Magickeeper tightened his mouth and refused to drink.

"Suit yourself. You leave me no choice. Any last words, you foolish boy?"

And Nick remembered the words, the spell.

Ochi chornyye, ochi strastnyye,
Ochi zhguchiye i prekrasnyye.
Kak lyublyu ya vas, kak boyus' ya vas,
Znat' uvidel vas ya v nedobryi chas.

The circle of his family. His last words were about that.
Rasputin could not turn him.

TATYANA RISES

SUDDENLY, THE CAVE SPARKLED. THE SNOWFLAKES GROWING on the wall twinkled.

Nick blinked as they flew from the walls, sparkling flakes blowing around the room. The cave was suddenly gleaming and bright, and the light formed a swirling funnel. Rasputin shielded his eyes. The Shadowkeepers squealed and shrunk back, some of them fleeing into other parts of the massive underground ice caves.

And in the middle of the light, Nick heard a voice. "You are the guardian, Nicholai. I knew you were the fulfiller of the prophecy, but I was frightened. I chose to hide you, but now I know you cannot hide such goodness."

The voice was his mother's!

"Lies!" Rasputin spat. He touched Nick's face and tried

to make the oily stuff slither into Nick's mouth, but it was now receding.

"This cannot be!" Rasputin howled.

"You cannot hide goodness, because it must shine a light in the darkness. I know that now, Kolya, my darling. And by choosing light and being willing to make the ultimate sacrifice, by invoking the spell of the family's protection, you have called all the light to you. All the good of the Magickeepers throughout history now resides in you. Guard it well, my love. Know that I am always with you."

Then the light filled the cave so brightly that Nick could not even see—but he could *feel*. He was no longer paralyzed, and he felt a strange flash—as if from his most intense Gaze ever—as the voice in the light poured into his chest.

Suddenly, Nick felt more powerful than he ever had in his entire life. The light faded from the room, and Nick saw that he was oil-free and shining himself.

He leaped from what, moments before, had been the stone bed where he was to die, and he took the monk by surprise. He called up fire and light into his hands, and hurled a flame—the largest he ever had seen—at Rasputin, who seemed weakened now that Tatyana had been there.

The monk screamed as his clothes caught on fire, and then he burst into flames.

Even in the fire, Nick heard him casting spells, trying to overcome what was happening.

The snowflakes still sparkled.

Nick stared at the flames as they shrank further and further until all that was left was a pile of ashes.

How true, Nick mused, that even those we think are the most powerful can be reduced to dust.

He exhaled. What had happened? What had really happened?

He stared down at the chalice. It was too powerful. He didn't even think it belonged in the vault.

First, he would save his father. Then he would destroy it.

CHAPTER
20

TATYANA'S GHOST

ICK EMERGED INSIDE HIS ROOM AND NEARLY CRIED WITH relief. Damian and Theo were there, along with Millie, her hand bandaged. Both his cousins had cuts and bruises, and their clothes were in shreds. When Nick opened the closet door, the two of them practically tackled him. "He isn't lost to us! Rejoice!" Theo cried out. "But how?" He looked down at the chalice in Nick's hand.

"I'll tell you later," Nick said, and ran to his father's bedside. His father's skin had turned a gray color, as if volcanic ash had settled there. Nick pressed his fingers to his father's icy cold neck. He felt a weak heartbeat.

They filled the chalice with water, which bubbled when it came in contact with the magical gold. Damian and Millie watched as Theo held up Nick's father's head. Nick held the chalice to his dad's mouth and poured the clear liquid between his frozen lips. Dribbles of water trickled down the corners of his mouth.

Nothing happened.

"Please, we've traveled so far and been through so much. This has to work."

But still his father was as ashen as a ghost.

Nick felt like a rock had settled in his throat. He tried to swallow, but it was as if his neck had twisted.

"Do it again," Damian commanded. "The magic will not fail us."

Nick held the chalice of water to his father's mouth. He poured a splash in, and again, much of it dribbled down his face.

"Look, Theo!"

Where the water trickled, the skin turned from gray to a fleshy pink.

"More!" Theo urged.

Nick pressed the chalice to his father's lips again and poured.

Slowly, as they watched, small signs of life returned. First, the very tips of his fingers turned back to a normal color, then his arms. His breathing, which had been so slow and shallow, grew more regular.

Nick poured more water into his father's mouth, and this time, his father appeared to swallow on his own.

Finally, his father's lips turned pinkish. He exhaled. Loudly.

They waited in silence, just listening for the sounds of his breathing.

Please, Nick urged in his mind. *Please, please, please, please wake up.*

And then his father's eyes fluttered open.

Nick had never seen such an awesome sight in his entire life.

"Kolya?" His father's voice was almost unrecognizable, more a rasp than anything else.

"It's me."

His dad smiled wanly. "Thank you."

Theo lowered his dad's head to the pillow. "You're going to need to rest for some time yet. Don't try to speak. Just rest. Rest. We'll leave you two alone…to catch up. Your son has had many an adventure in the search for this chalice that saved you."

Theo, Damian, and Millie left the room and shut the door. Nick sat on the edge of the bed. "I thought you were going to die," he said softly. At the words, his shoulders shuddered slightly. Then, in a tumble, Nick started to explain everything that had happened, from the trip to England, to Howard Hughes, to Shakespeare, to clouds, to Amelia Earhart.

"You saved me," his father whispered.

"I had to. You never asked to be part of this world."

"But for you, I will be. For her, I would be. I heard music," his father said. "It was the song she always sang to you. I heard the notes. And I heard your mother's voice."

"I played the music box for you." Nick pointed to the bedside table. "I wanted you to feel like I was here. Like *she* was here. It's her music box. Everything in my room belonged to her when she was a girl." He glanced at his Tony Hawk poster and grinned. "Well, *almost* everything."

His father sat up, gasping, "No...no, you don't understand, Kolya. She *was* here."

Nick patted him on his chest and said, "Dad...rest." He couldn't even imagine what his father had been through.

His father leaned his head back on the pillow. Strands of his hair were still falling out. Nick knew it would be a long time until his dad was totally well.

"I know she was here, Nick. The whole time. I heard you. When you came into this room, I heard you. And I was aware I was someplace very dark. And very, very cold. But—I wasn't in pain. Not sharp pain. It was more that I wanted to be free of that place. I wanted my struggle to be over. I was neither dead nor alive. So I was frightened. But the whole time I was in that place, she talked to me. She told me not to lose hope, not to fall into the darkness. She whispered to me—this voice. Her voice. It was so *good* to hear her voice, Kolya. It was just as I remembered it."

"I don't believe in ghosts, Dad."

"But you do believe in magic."

Nick whispered solemnly, "More than ever. I know she was here. Because where I was…I saw her and heard her too."

Nick stared at the chalice on the nightstand. Its magic had saved his dad's life. Now it was time to ensure that no one else ever came into possession of the chalice.

"I need to take care of something, Dad. Tonight. But I promise I'll be back to tell you what happened." He turned to leave, then faced his dad again. "I love you."

BACK TO THE BEGINNING

*T*HE THREE COUSINS STOOD IN THE MIDDLE OF THE EGYPTIAN desert. A moon hung in a cavernous sky with stars stretching for eternity.

Nick shivered. "How can it be so hot during the day and so cold at night?"

"If you would study, you would know the answer to this," Theo teased.

Nick noticed that his cousins' bruises were still visible from their fight with the Shadowkeepers. They had been outnumbered, but fighting together, they had slain the minions with a combination of spells and fighting skills.

Damian held up the chalice. "Are we sure of this?" he asked.

Theo nodded solemnly.

"Kolya? You are sure?"

Nick nodded, too.

"Then the location of the chalice will be known only to the three of us. We each solemnly vow never to reveal it. Now, let us place our hands on it," Damian commanded.

When the three of them all touched the stem of the chalice, a light glowed from it, as brilliant as sunshine and spreading upward, like a beacon.

"What's going on?" Nick breathed, squinting.

"When the chalice was created, it was by the three most powerful Magickeepers, the originators of the bloodline. Now, we three are the most powerful in the world. We will bury it, safe in the sands of time, at its point of origin far below the earth, guarded by the spirits of our ancestors, where it has belonged all this time. Our power will create the shield around it. Our power will ensure the chalice never sees the world again."

Together, the three of them formed a circle, and with their minds, they pulled the beam of light downward. Nick had never tried to control such energy before. It was like containing a hurricane in a tea cup.

He concentrated, feeling himself united with Theo and Damian in a way he had never been before—as their equal, not just as their little cousin. He had trained with them, learned from them, but he now knew that his actual power, what he had been born with, was as strong as theirs.

Together, the three of them focused until all the light was again contained in the chalice, and then, in a final burst of flames, it disappeared from their hands and shot down into the sand, creating a gaping hole. The three of them almost slipped in it—and Nick knew when he had seen a spell like that before: when Rasputin made Madame Bogdanovich's shop disappear.

They fell to the desert floor and scrambled backward. Then Damian rose up in the air, commanding the sands, which flew in a whirlwind around them before settling down.

"Look," Nick pointed as his cousin alit on the ground again. The desert floor was undisturbed.

"And there it shall remain, in the sands of our origin," Damian pronounced.

"May it never be uncovered," Theo said.

CELEBRATION

*W*HEN THE THREE OF THEM RETURNED TO THE WINTER Palace, the family was waiting. They looked like they were mourning.

"What's wrong?" he asked Isabella, who was crying uncontrollably into Sascha's furry neck. She looked up, and at the sight of him, she began shrieking.

"Nick! Nick! Nick!"

Around him, a huge cheer went up.

"We thought you were lost to us forever," said Irina. She kissed him on both cheeks. Then she eyed Damian and Theo up and down. "I take it you did not get these bruises from playing badminton."

Damian shook his head. "It's been a very long night."

They all went into the dining room, and then Nick

recounted what had happened in the cave. He thought they might think he'd imagined what happened—with Tatyana's ghost and the light and the defeat of Rasputin. He looked down at the Grand Duchess. She nodded. "There is one thing I have learned having lived a long, long time, Kolya. The ones we love never truly die."

Theo nodded. "We have ensured that the chalice will never again be used by those unknowing of its power. It is hidden forever, as it should be."

Damian signaled, and platters of food arrived. Someone started playing the balalaika. Damian stood on top of the table and tapped his boot and clapped his hands, beginning a Russian folk dance. Irina rose up and joined him. His father was even there, looking tired but laughing next to Grandpa. The Grand Duchess was beaming, her two tigers by her side.

There was dancing and music and joy and laughter. Nick was enjoying himself so much, he didn't even notice that Theo had excused himself at some point in the evening.

Nick left the dining room and slipped down the hall to Theo's classroom. He found his cousin writing in the book—*the Book*—where all of the family's history was recorded.

"What are you doing, Theo? Don't you want to be with us?"

"I wanted to record the events while they were fresh in my mind."

"What did you write? Can I see?"

Theo scowled at him. "I think not. History…is best left in the book, and life is best lived in the moment."

"But why is it so important? Why do you record everything?"

"So we learn. From our mistakes. From our victories. From our celebrations."

"What did you write about me?"

Theo sighed. He took off his glasses. Nick could see that aside from the bruises and scratches from his battle, Theo's eyes were worried and a little sad. Theo cleaned his glasses, put them back on his nose, pushed them up, turned a page, and began reading aloud.

"Today, in an act of selflessness, a new prince of the Magickeepers was born. For only the wise and the brave know that immortality is not a blessing but a curse. And only the wise and the brave would sacrifice their own lives for others."

Nick stared at his cousin. "Was my mother really in that cave?"

Theo nodded. "And now…all of the power of your entire lineage courses through you. On your thirteenth birthday, those months ago, you learned about the world of magic. You learned who you are and where you came from."

Nick thought back to that night. It seemed so long ago.

"But," Theo continued, "tonight, in the ice caves beneath

Mother Russia and in the sands of our ancestors, you, Nicholai Rostov, Prince of the Magickeepers, became a man."

Nick exhaled. He knew it was true.

A Prince of the Magickeepers and all the responsibility it entailed.

As his cousins had reminded him from the first day he met them: This was his destiny.

RELIVE NICK ROSTOV'S THRILLING JOURNEY

AND DISCOVER THE SPECTACULAR SECRETS OF

THE MAGICKEEPERS

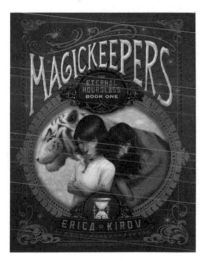

The Eternal Hourglass
978-1-4022-3855-0

The Pyramid of Souls
978-1-4022-1502-3

ABOUT THE AUTHOR

 ERICA KIROV is an American writer of Russian descent. She lives in Virginia with her family and a large menagerie of pets. She cannot play the balalaika, but she does enjoy a blini from time to time. She is hard at work on her next novel and may be reached at www.magickeepers.com.